AF490542

For My Family
        And My Friends
            Thank you!

Chapter 1

Isabela San Pedro walked rapidly down the hallway of the high school. Her work shoes whispered softly against the carpeted floor. She glanced at her watch. Taking the detour to the high school had thrown her off schedule, but if she hurried, she could still be on time for work.

Ordinarily, Isabela would have just told her daughter Alicia that she needed to be more responsible and that she'd just have to do without her band instrument for a day. However, Alicia had been selected to play in an Honor Band in Idaho, and the band teacher wanted to work with all of the Honor Band students during music period, so Alicia needed her oboe.

As Isabela exited the front door of the school, the cold, January air took her breath away for just a moment. Large flakes of snow were swirling through the air. The flakes were almost rain, but not quite.

As she neared the parking lot, a sudden gust of wind caught a strand of her long dark hair, flipping it into her face. With her hands buried deep in her pockets, Isabela tried unsuccessfully to move the hair by shaking her head.

As she did so, she stepped off the curb into the parking lot. Suddenly, out of nowhere, a red SUV rounded the corner. It swerved to avoid colliding with Isabela but managed to hit a deep puddle of slush. Dirty, icy water splattered all over Isabela.

The SUV paused and the driver's side window rolled down. A dark-haired man poked his head through the window.

"Hey, a little courtesy would be nice!" Isabela called to him. "It's a parking lot, not a racetrack."

"Watch where you're going!" the driver yelled back. "You stepped in front of me!"

Isabela didn't bother to reply. She could see no point in arguing with this overbearing man. For just a moment, she wished her mother hadn't taught her to always act like a lady because she had the overwhelming urge to flip the man off. However, her mother's teachings prevailed. Isabela just shook her head in disgust and hurried to her car.

As she unlocked the doors to her minivan, she gazed dismally down at her soaked uniform. So much for being on time for work. Now she would need to run home and change into new scrubs and different work shoes before she reported to work at the care center.

Twenty minutes later, Isabela was clocking in for her shift. She was only ten minutes late, but it was the second time in two weeks that she had been late for work. Zoe, the charge nurse, gave Isabela a dirty look as Isabela studied the schedule to see which patients she would be in charge of for the day.

"It's nice of you to decide to show up," said Zoe sarcastically.

Isabela tried not to let Zoe's negative attitude bother her too much because Zoe was always grumpy. As charge nurse, Zoe had the responsibility to decide who was in charge of which patients and to deal with any minor difficulties the nurses might run into throughout the day, but she didn't have the authority to place anyone on probation or fire them.

Isabela quickly grabbed her patients' charts and began going to the various rooms to check on each of them, to see how they were doing. She loved her job. She enjoyed visiting with the various patients, even the grumpy ones.

In fact, she loved it when she had a grouchy patient. She always took it as a personal challenge to find a way to cheer up that person's sour demeanor. Nine times out of ten she was successful. Nothing was more satisfying than seeing a smile or getting a bit of a laugh out of someone who was hurting and angry.

Isabela paused outside Mr. Weaver's door. He was one of her favorite patients, and she was delighted that he was on her list for the day. Mr. Weaver had a no-nonsense attitude that Isabela loved.

"Good morning, Mr. Weaver," she said cheerfully as she entered his room.

"Bob," said the old man from his wheelchair. "How many times do I have to tell you to call me Bob?"

"A million and one," laughed Isabela.

"How's my favorite nurse?" asked Bob.

"I'll step out and see if I can find her," replied Isabela as she took her stethoscope and listened to Bob's heart.

Bob chuckled appreciatively. "Isabela," he said, "when are you going to find yourself a nice man and settle down?"

"I'm too busy with work and my daughter to worry about finding a man," replied Isabela as she adjusted a blood pressure cuff on the old man's upper arm.

"You should never be too busy to find someone to share your life with," Bob advised. "Before you know it, that daughter of yours will be out of the house, and you'll be all alone. Find a guy, Isabela. You'll be glad you did."

"I'm holding out for a guy who's as nice as you are," laughed Isabela as she put away the blood pressure cuff.

"Don't be so picky," Bob joined in her laughter.

Isabela stepped out of the room and went down the hall to her next patient. Sometimes she wished she really could follow Bob's advice to find a nice guy, but there weren't a lot of single guys in her age group in Richfield. And she needed to be picky. She didn't want to end up with another disaster like her first husband.

She tried to think back to the last time she'd met a man. The answer made her chuckle softly to herself. The last time she'd met anyone even remotely in her age group was that overbearing man in the parking lot who almost ran over her. Of course, she didn't really meet him. They hadn't even exchanged names.

"Even if I did know who he was, I would never want to date someone like him," Isabela told herself as she entered the next room. Although, deep down, part of her had to admit that even during the confrontation, she'd noticed that the man was rather handsome.

Isabela was just finishing up her morning checks when she received a text. The message was from Alicia. *Can you chaperone our Honor Band trip?*

Chaperone Honor Band? Isabela was both horrified and flattered by the idea. She was honored that Alicia would want her to tag along on a school trip. It would be fun to see Alicia interacting with her friends, and she would also get to see the concert. On the other hand, chaperoning a bunch of teenagers on an overnight trip seemed a little overwhelming. Still, she liked to be supportive of her daughter, and she was sure it was difficult for the band teacher to find parents willing to go on overnight trips.

What are the dates? She texted back. *I'll need to see if I can get it off work.*

After a brief pause, Alicia replied, *Jan. 9, 10, and 11.*

You're not giving me much notice, Isabela responded.

Sorry. Just found out he needs a female chaperone for the trip. Let me know ASAP.

Okay, Isabela texted. *I'll know in a couple of hours.*

Phone in hand, Isabela went and checked the schedule for the following week. She already had the 10th and 11th off. If she could find someone to trade shifts with her, then she would be able to chaperone the trip. As she glanced up from the schedule, she saw Molly heading towards her.

Molly! She was the perfect person to ask. Molly was single and didn't usually have a lot of plans that were set in stone. Besides, Isabela had covered a couple of Molly's shifts over Thanksgiving.

"Hey, Molly!" called Isabela. "I need a huge favor!"

"What is it?" asked Molly. She walked over to Isabela with a big smile on her freckled face. Her red hair was pulled back in a bun, but even pulled back her hair still showed signs of being curly.

"Can you either trade a shift with me or cover for me? I need January ninth off, so I can chaperone a school trip with Alicia."

"Oh, that sounds like fun!" exclaimed Molly. "Am I already off that day?"

"Yes," replied Isabela. "Can you trade?"

"Let's look at the schedule," said Molly.

She led Isabela back to the calendar that was hanging on the wall of the employee break room. The women studied the schedule for a few seconds before Molly spoke.

"I work the eighth, but that's my little niece's first birthday. How about if we trade the eighth and the ninth? I get to go to the party, and you get to chaperone the trip."

"That sounds great," said Isabela happily. "I'll put in the trade request."

After Molly left, Isabela pulled her cell phone out of the pocket of her scrubs and texted Alicia back. *I'm good to go. I have all three days off. Tell Mr. Jacob's I can do it if he still needs me.*

He does, Alicia replied in just a few seconds. *He'll email you all of the details.*

Isabela slipped her phone back into her pocket and went to check on another patient. She realized she was excited about the trip. It would give her a chance to spend more time with her daughter. Alicia was only a freshman in high school. In fact, she wouldn't turn fifteen for a couple more months, but already Isabela was beginning to dread the day when Alicia left home for good. Even though Alicia still had another three years of high school, Isabela knew that the time would fly by quickly.

The day had started out kind of rocky after her run-in with the overbearing jerk in the parking lot, but things were starting to look up now. Chaperoning a music trip to Idaho might not sound like fun to a lot of people, but Isabela found she was actually looking forward to it. After all, what could possibly go wrong?

Chapter 2

The band students left right after school on Thursday evening. A surprising number of students had made it into the Honor Band which was being held in Rexburg, Idaho on the campus of Brigham Young University Idaho. While they waited in the band room for the bus to come, Alicia explained that sometimes only one or two students were chosen for the Honor Band, but the school's band director had been working hard with the students since the beginning of the year. Several had auditioned, and almost all of them had been selected, including Alicia and her best friend Alejandro Varilla.

Alicia had just finished explaining the auditioning process to Isabela when a tall, handsome young man approached them. He was grinning from ear to ear. His dark hair was cut short, emphasizing his big brown eyes and tan skin. He was a touch darker than Alicia and Isabela, but not much.

"Uhhh-leesh-uh!" he drawled as he approached. He grinned at how well he had anglicized the pronunciation of Alicia's name. "Are you ready for this thing."

"Alley-jan-droh," replied Alicia, butchering her friend's name as much as possible. "I am more ready than you are because I actually practiced my instrument."

"If you practiced, then why does your horn sound like a dying cat?" asked the boy good-naturedly.

"Ouch," responded Alicia with a laugh. "If it sounds like a dying cat, it's only because your squeaking clarinet is killing us both."

The boy started laughing and then gave Alicia a quick hug. For a moment, Isabela wondered if the two kids were actually dating, even though Alicia always insisted that she didn't have a boyfriend.

"Mom, this is Alejandro," she said, pronouncing his name correctly as she introduced him.

"Oh!" said Isabela in surprise. "This is the Alejandro you're always talking to?"

"Yes," laughed Alicia. "Why do you sound so shocked?"

"For some reason, I expected someone shorter and younger," replied Isabela with a shrug. "You're always so mean to him when I hear you talking on the phone that I just figured he must be a little kid."

"See, Alicia," spoke up Alejandro, "even your mom recognizes that you need to be nicer to me." He grinned as he spoke.

Isabela was gratified to hear him pronounce Alicia's name correctly. For some reason, it always bothered her when people used the English pronunciation, rather than saying it Ah-lees-ee-ah. Of course, perhaps that was because she was always being called Izabella, rather than Ees-ah-bel-ah. It was even worse when someone called her Izzy. Isabela realized she was being fanatical, but when it came to names, she felt it was important to say them right and spell them correctly. At work, she had been complimented more than once by patients for getting their names right. She felt it was a matter of respect, and everyone deserved to be respected enough to have their names pronounced correctly.

"The bus is here!" someone announced excitedly.

A general bustle followed as students gathered up overnight bags and instruments and headed outside to board the school bus parked near the band room. Mr. Jacobs, the band director, stood near the door of the bus ticking off names on a sheet as each student boarded the bus. When he saw Isabela, he smiled broadly.

"Ms. San Pedro, thanks for agreeing to come with us," he said.

"Just call me Isabela. Ms. San Pedro sounds way too formal and way too old. I feel like a grandma when you call me that," she told him.

"You'd better get used to feeling old then," chuckled Mr. Jacobs. "All the students will have to refer to you as Ms. San Pedro. They are required to call chaperones by Mr. or Ms. It's a school policy."

"I'll accept it from them, but you can call me Isabela. Where do you want me to sit?"

"I have two seats reserved for the chaperones in the middle of the bus," replied Mr. Jacobs. "You can have one of those seats all to yourself. You and our other chaperone will be separating the boys and the girls."

"Separating the boys and the girls?" Isabela raised her eyebrows in confusion.

"Another school policy. After dark, the boys and the girls have to be separated. Since it will be dark in another hour or so, I decided to just separate them to begin with. We have boys in the back and girls in the front with the chaperones' seats separating them."

"Who's the other chaperone?" asked Isabela.

"Javier Varilla," replied Mr. Jacobs. "Alejandro Varilla's father. Alicia and Alejandro are my music reps this quarter, so they were in charge of getting chaperones. They took the easy way out by volunteering their own parents."

"Such lovely children," laughed Isabela as she got ready to board the bus. "Well, it will be nice to meet Alejandro's father. I'm sure he's a nice man if he's anything like his son."

Isabela repositioned her backpack on her shoulder and climbed onto the bus. She stood for a moment in the center of the aisle and gazed around the bus. Halfway back she could see an empty seat with a "RESERVED" sign taped to the back of the seat. Across the aisle, a man was already seated. He was looking backwards at the students behind him. After a moment, Isabela realized he was talking to Alejandro.

Isabela hurried down the aisle, anxious to meet the other chaperone. She wondered if he had gone on any other trips like this. Since it was her first time chaperoning, she hoped that he had a little experience and would be able to help her be more effective in her role.

Isabela placed her backpack in her seat next to the window and settled down. With a large smile on her face, she turned to introduce herself to Mr. Varilla. The man seated next to her was staring at her in surprise. If his face had not been marred with a frown, he would have looked very handsome. He had the same dark hair, brown eyes, and tanned skin as his son. His jaw was angular, and Isabela could see he was quite muscular, even though he had on a jacket.

However, it wasn't the frown on his face nor the muscles bulging under his hoodie that caught her attention. She recognized him immediately. It was the crazy driver from the parking lot a few days before; the driver who had splashed her with freezing water.

"You!" she said accusingly. "*You're* the other chaperone?"

"Sadly, yes," he replied coldly. "Believe me; I'm not any happier about this than you are. If I had known you would be the other chaperone, I would have refused to come."

"You wouldn't have needed to do that. I would have declined the invitation if I'd known that I'd be dealing with you for the next few days," replied Isabela.

"It's too late now for either one of us to back out," said Mr. Varilla. Isabela noticed he had just a trace of an accent. English wasn't his first language.

"I know," she said in resignation. "We'll just have to agree to play nice in the sandbox."

"I will if you will," he told her. "Just watch where you're going. I don't want to have to worry about you getting run over by any cars."

"Since none of the drivers will be you, I don't think that will be a worry," Isabela responded tightly. "Most adults already know how to drive."

Before Mr. Varilla could respond, she turned her back to him and dug a paperback book out of her backpack. She was glad she'd decided to pack a couple extra books to read. She could tell already it was going to be a long trip.

Chapter 3

Almost three hours later, the bus was driving through the traffic of Salt Lake City. Mr. Jacob's stood up at the front of the bus.

"Hey, Band!" he called to get everyone's attention.

"Hey, what?" the kids called back.

"We're going to stop in a few minutes to get something to eat. The place we're stopping at has a lot of food options but be quick. You only have thirty minutes. We want to try to get to Rexburg before midnight."

Mr. Jacobs sat back down. About ten minutes later, the bus pulled off the freeway and parked next to a popular fast-food restaurant. Isabela stepped off the bus and gazed around her. She didn't care for fast food. It always made her feel sluggish and upset her stomach a little. To her relief, next to one of the hamburger places was a little sandwich shop that served deli sandwiches. This was something she could eat.

"Hey, Mom," called Alicia. "Where are you going to eat?" Alicia was surrounded by four other girls.

"Probably that little sandwich shop," replied Isabela, pointing in the direction of the restaurant.

"Okay, wait for me!" said Alicia. She turned and said something to the other girls before leaving them and joining Isabela.

"You could have eaten with your friends," protested Isabela. "I'm fine alone."

"Well, if you don't want me," replied Alicia, pretending to be hurt.

"Of course, I want you to eat with me," laughed Isabela, "but I don't want you to feel like you can't eat with your friends just because I'm here."

"I'd rather eat with you," confessed Alicia. "Those girls can get kind of annoying."

Alicia led the way across the parking lot to the sandwich shop. Isabela was pleased to see that hardly anyone was inside. Most of the students had opted for burgers and fries. That meant she wouldn't have to feel rushed about getting her food. She and Alicia stepped up to the counter. They ordered a large roast beef sandwich on whole wheat. The sandwiches were big enough that they decided they could split one, and both be satisfied.

Isabela was just paying for the sandwich when she felt a gust of cold air hit her as the door opened. She glanced over her shoulder. Mr. Varilla and his son stepped into the shop. She had planned on eating the sandwich at one of the tables in the establishment, but the sight of Mr. Varilla instantly changed her mind. She didn't want to even be in the same room as him.

Unfortunately, their kids had different plans. "Alley-jan-droh!" exclaimed Alicia, "come and eat with us." Before Isabela could protest, Alicia was moving their drinks from the small round table she'd selected to a larger booth.

"Do we have time to even eat here?" asked Mr. Varilla. He eyed Isabela coldly. Apparently, he wasn't any more keen to eat with her than she was with him.

"I'm sure we do," replied Alejandro. "We still have twenty minutes. Besides, the bus isn't going to leave the chaperones. Mr. Jacobs doesn't want to be stuck all alone with a bunch of teenagers."

"Maybe we should eat on the bus anyway, just to be safe," said Mr. Varilla.

"No, come and eat with us. Alejandro and I can't even talk to each other because of having the boys and girls separated," spoke up Alicia.

"All right," sighed Alejandro's father.

He stepped up to the counter with his son and ordered a large sandwich for himself and one for Alejandro. Once their sandwiches were made, the pair came over and joined Isabela and Alicia.

"So, how is it being chaperones?" asked Alicia as the group unwrapped their sandwiches.

"So far, not bad," replied Mr. Varilla. He eyed Isabela suspiciously, as though he suspected she would be the source of all their troubles.

"The kids seem pretty well-behaved," volunteered Isabela. She glared back at Mr. Varilla to let him know that she felt the students had better manners than he did.

"Mr. Jacobs says that the Honor Band trips are the best trips because all the kids who go are serious about music. They aren't on a trip to miss school, but to really improve their music skills," said Alejandro.

"That makes sense," Isabela replied.

She took a small bite of her sandwich. Across the table, she saw Mr. Varilla take a huge bite out of his own sandwich. The action reminded her of an alligator snapping after its prey. For some reason, the action made the man seem even more aggravating. She glanced at her watch. They only had about ten minutes left.

"Maybe we should go get on the bus," she suggested. "We might not get left, but I don't want to set a bad example either."

"Mom, we're fine," said Alicia.

"I'm sure we can spare another five minutes," spoke up Mr. Varilla. His voice was deep and almost musical, which for some reason, made Isabela feel even more irritated with him.

Rather than reply, Isabela smiled tightly and took another bite of her sandwich. Alicia and Alejandro began talking about the bus ride and who was the most annoying in their sections of the bus.

"The two boys in the very back of the bus keep cussing," complained Alejandro. "I don't really care that much personally, but they're saying a lot of really foul things because they're trying to make Robert mad."

"Who's Robert?" asked Isabela.

"He's one of the sweetest boys in the band," spoke up Alicia. "He has autism. His mom told me that he's highly functioning autistic. Anyway, he plays the trumpet, and he's really good at it. He struggles in a lot of classes, but not in band. He's like this trumpet progidy or something."

"Prodigy," corrected Alejandro with a grin. "She always says it wrong."

"Whatever," laughed Alicia. "Anyway, he's really nice. He has this definite sense of right and wrong, and he gets mad when people cross that line. So, if the boys in the back are cussing just to cuss, he's going to get really upset. And then it will be hard to calm him down."

"What kind of upset?" Isabela asked in a concerned voice. "He won't try to fight them, will he?"

"Oh, no!" said Alejandro. "Not like that. His feelings will get hurt or something. He'll end up getting so frustrated with them that he'll probably start crying."

"It's so sad," Alicia added. "This is his first school trip without his mom chaperoning. He was so proud about getting to go without her. I really want him to have fun. Those boys are going to ruin everything."

"Not if I can help it," spoke up Isabela firmly. "Tell me which boys, and I'll speak to them."

"It might be better if Alejandro's dad says something instead," said Alicia. "They're senior boys. I think they'll just laugh at you and say you're being overly sensitive because you're a girl."

"I'd like to see them say that to my face," said Isabela hotly.

"They'll say it behind your back, and it will make Robert upset all over again," explained Alejandro. "Alicia's right. It's better if my dad says something."

"I see," said Isabela reluctantly. "Are you willing to say something to the boys, Mr. Varilla?"

"Yes, but only on one condition," replied Alejandro's dad.

"You have a condition for doing your job?" Isabela questioned in disbelief.

"Only one. You can't call me Mr. Varilla anymore. It makes me feel like I'm older than my father. Just call me Javier."

"Agreed," said Isabela, "but only because I told Mr. Jacobs not to call me Ms. San Pedro. I feel like I should get out my walker and hearing aid when I hear that."

The comment drew smiles from everyone at the table, including Javier, which had an unsettling effect on Isabela. For some reason, she hadn't noticed how handsome he was until he smiled his wide grin, which revealed a small dimple in his left cheek and made his eyes light up. Isabela couldn't help but think that it was too bad that his personality wasn't as attractive as his looks.

Chapter 4

When they re-entered the bus, Isabela was pleased to see Javier go directly to the very back of the bus and sit down on one of the empty seats. He engaged in a conversation with the two boys who had been cussing. Curiously, she watched the interaction to see if he would be angry and threatening with them or if he would just sternly warn them. To her surprise, she saw him laughing and joking with the boys. After a few minutes, his countenance sobered. She could tell he was speaking seriously to the pair. They immediately became more serious and nodded their heads in agreement. Once the interaction was over, Javier shook hands with both boys and returned to his seat. He caught Isabela watching him. She tried to look away, but it was too late.

"They agreed to stop cussing," said Javier in answer to her unspoken question.

"What did you say to them?" she asked curiously. "I saw you guys laughing."

"We were just joking around about how much fun it is to ride for hours on a bus with nothing to do. They said they like to sleep. I told them that when I sleep all cramped up in a bus, I feel like I've aged thirty years, and it's not a good look on me." Javier grinned boyishly. Isabela couldn't help but notice once again how attractive his smile was.

"They probably thought that was funny," said Isabela.

"They did. Then I just told them that reports of them cussing had reached my ears, and I would appreciate it if they wouldn't cuss, especially since we have someone who is special needs with us. I was up front and honest with them. I told them it was a pretty big deal for Robert to get to come on this trip without a parent, and my job as chaperone was to make sure he had a positive experience. I said that since they are two of the oldest boys on the bus, I'd appreciate it if they could just kind of keep an eye out for Robert, make sure no one is bullying him or harassing him. They agreed. Hopefully, it works."

He shrugged his shoulders. Isabela could tell he was uncertain his approach was the right way to handle it, but she was impressed with the clever way he had taken care of the situation.

"I think that was a good way to put it," she told him. "They seem like nice boys. They probably just needed things explained to them."

"True," agreed Javier. "And then some people just don't have common sense when it comes to certain situations, and they have to have it spelled out for them." He stared pointedly at Isabela as he spoke.

Isabela felt herself prickle at the statement. Was he referring to her in the parking lot? If he was, he had a lot of nerve since he was the one tearing through the parking lot like he was in a race. Before she could confront him, he had turned his attention to something outside the window. She stared at the back of his broad shoulders and continued to fume. He could be quite pleasant when he wanted to, but then he would do something irritating. He was one of the most aggravating people she had ever met.

Chapter 5

For the remainder of the bus ride, Isabela made it a point to ignore Javier. She talked to several of the kids on the bus, trying to get to know them so she could be a more effective chaperone. One girl in particular caught her attention. The girl was dressed in all black. Her hair was obviously dyed black; Isabela could see her blonde roots. She had a piercing on her eyebrow and wore heavy black makeup.

"I don't think I've met you," said Isabela, sitting next to the girl. "I'm trying to get to know everyone's names."

"I'm Miranda," said the girl.

"I'm Ms. San Pedro, Alicia's mom, in case you hadn't figured that out," replied Isabela. "What grade are you in?"

"I'm a junior," replied Miranda.

Isabela wrinkled her forehead, perplexed. "I really don't recognize you," she admitted to the girl. "I'm sorry, but I'm trying to remember you. What instrument do you play?"

"The flute," said Miranda.

"The flute?" said Isabela. "Oh, dear, now I really feel dumb. The flutes sit on the front row. I should recognize you from the concerts, but I don't."

"Well," Miranda replied with a sigh, "I didn't have my hair dyed black during the Christmas concert; plus, I just moved here at Thanksgiving, so that's probably why you don't know me."

"Oh, that explains a lot," laughed Isabela. "Where did you live before you came to Richfield?"

"Arizona," replied Miranda. "I'm not used to the cold or the small town. I grew up in Phoenix."

"I'll bet it's a culture shock to you," empathized Isabela. "What brought your family to Richfield?"

"Just me," said Miranda. Her face closed off. "Family issues. I'm here living with my aunt."

"Oh." Isabela squirmed uncomfortably. She hadn't meant to open any wounds with the girl, but it was obvious Miranda was not happy about being in Richfield. "Who's your aunt?"

"Zoe Barnes. She works as a nurse at the care center."

"Zoe? I know Zoe. She and I work together," said Isabela.

Miranda's interest in the conversation picked back up. "You work with my aunt?"

"Yes, I do. We work the day shift together," replied Isabela.

"Is she as annoying at work as she is at home?" asked Miranda. "She's always grumpy, which is weird because she used to be cool, but not anymore. She's just always angry about something."

Isabela bit her lower lip. She didn't want to say anything negative about Zoe to Miranda, even though Zoe sometimes seemed to go out of her way to make Isabela's life miserable. Come to think of it though, Zoe hadn't always been such a grump. It was only the past few months that she had been so grouchy. Isabela wondered if it had anything to do with the family problems Zoe had mentioned.

"She's an excellent nurse," said Isabela truthfully. "She works as Charge Nurse quite a bit, and her patients really like her. Maybe she's just tired when she's home. She's a hard worker."

"Maybe," replied Miranda doubtfully.

Isabela could tell the conversation was over, so she moved on to another seat and a pair of girls who were laughing and giggling about something. However, Isabela couldn't help but wonder what sort of family problems had brought Miranda all the way from Phoenix, Arizona to Richfield, Utah.

She wanted to ask Mr. Jacobs what he knew but decided against it. Her mother had always taught her that a fine line existed between curiosity and wanting to know something because you truly cared about the person.

Isabela's mom told her, "Don't try to find out about someone unless your heart is in the right place. Otherwise, you're just being nosy."

Isabela returned to her seat to ponder the conversation she'd had with Miranda. Did she need to know why Miranda was here? Or was she just being nosy? Until Isabela knew what was behind her own motives, she decided she should mind her own business…but even so, a little voice in the back of her head kept telling her she should learn more about the mysterious Miranda.

Chapter 6

It was almost midnight when the bus pulled into the parking lot of the hotel where the group would be staying. A few of the kids stirred to get off the bus, but Mr. Jacobs stopped them

"Everyone wait here," he said. "I'll go in and get our room keys. Sit tight until I get back."

The kids settled back down. Isabela glanced over at Javier. He looked in her direction at the same time and caught her eye. He grinned mockingly at her and raised an eyebrow. Isabela looked quickly away, embarrassed. She didn't want him to think that she felt any feelings towards him because she didn't. Even though she knew from conversations with Alicia that Alejandro's father was single, she had no interest in him whatsoever.

Mr. Jacobs arrived shortly and called for everyone's attention. "Hey, Band!"

"Hey, what?" the kids chorused back.

"The hotel serves breakfast, so we'll eat here in the morning. We have to be at the university at 8:30 for registration. Rehearsals begin at 9:00. That means we are leaving the hotel at 8:15. Don't be late. Be sure to take your instruments off the bus tonight. It's too cold to leave them out here. Lights out and room checks will be at 12:30, so in a half hour. Now listen up while I give you room assignments."

As each group of students was called, they gathered their stuff and headed off the bus. Isabela could hear clattering underneath the bus as suitcases were pulled out and rearranged while students searched for luggage and instruments. Finally, her own name was called. As the only female chaperone, she would have her own room.

"At 12:30, meet me in the lobby," Mr. Jacob's told her. "I'll need your help with the room checks."

He handed her a hotel key and a sheet of paper with the list of rooms and who was in each room. She glanced down at the list. A flash of annoyance passed through her to see that Javier was only two rooms down from her. That would make it even harder for her to avoid him.

Isabela pulled her backpack over her shoulder a little more firmly and walked down the stairs of the bus.

She stood next to the side of the bus and surveyed the stack of luggage that the bus driver and some of the older boys had made. She located her suitcase and picked it up. It was heavier than she remembered it being, and she struggled to get a good grip on the handle.

Suddenly, a man's hand reached down and took it from her. Glancing up she saw that it was Javier. He smiled boldly down at her. She hadn't realized how much taller he was than her. She was 5'4", and he easily had eight or nine inches on her.

"I can do it," she protested.

"I know you can," he said, "but my abuela always taught me to help carry luggage. You can't argue with a grandma."

"That's true," agreed Isabela with a laugh. She relinquished her hold on the suitcase.

The parking lot had been plowed of snow, but it was still slick, and Isabela was glad that she didn't have to try to keep her balance while holding onto the suitcase and her backpack. When Javier deposited her suitcase just inside the door of her room, she thanked him warmly before stepping inside.

The room was a standard hotel room with two queen-sized beds and a flatscreen television mounted to the wall.

Isabela crossed the room and looked out the window. Large hills of snow lined the streets. It was obvious that Rexburg received more snow that Richfield. She reached down and turned on the heat to dispel the chill in the room while she picked out the clothes that she would wear the following day.

Isabela stifled a large yawn. She glanced down at her watch. It was almost time to meet Mr. Jacobs and Javier in the lobby for room checks. She decided that she may as well go down early. She would rather be the first one there than have them waiting on her.

When she arrived, she was surprised to see that Javier was already there. He was seated in one of the chairs next to the glass fireplace. He was reading a local newspaper that he had picked up from one of the end tables.

Isabela came and sat down on the couch. "Anything interesting in the news?" she asked.

"Not really," he shook his head. "This weekend the university is hosting a high school honor band, but I guess we already knew that."

Isabela chuckled softly. "I've heard rumors."

Javier yawned broadly. "Sorry," he said shaking his head. "I'm too old for this late-night stuff."

Before Isabela could reply, Mr. Jacobs came and sat down on the other end of the couch from Isabela. He had the list of the kids and the rooms they were in.

"Are you ready to do room checks?" he asked tiredly.

"Mr. Jacobs, you look exhausted," spoke up Isabela. "Do you want Javier and me to just do it?"

"Sure, tell us what to do. We'll take care of it," agreed Javier.

"I would really appreciate that if you don't mind," said Mr. Jacobs. "I've been up since four getting the final arrangements made for this trip."

"No problem," said Isabela with a smile. "What do we do?"

"Did you bring your room lists?" asked Mr. Jacobs.

"I have mine," spoke up Javier. He pulled a folded sheet of paper out of the breast pocket of his button-down shirt.

"Great," said Mr. Jacobs. "You just go to each room and knock on the door. You make sure that the four kids listed on the sheet are in the room and that there are no extras. Then tell the kids it's lights out and no one is allowed out of their rooms until morning."

"That's it?" said Javier. "I thought it would be more difficult than that."

"It's pretty easy, but some of the rooms you will have to actually do a roll call to make sure," said Mr. Jacobs.

"How will we know which rooms need that?" asked Isabela.

"You'll know," said Mr. Jacobs mysteriously. Then he laughed. "If the room seems wild, do a roll call. If they already seem settled down for the night, you can skip it and just ask the kids if everyone's there."

"Okay," said Isabela. "Anything else we need to do?"

"I hate to ask," replied Mr. Jacobs, "but if you don't mind staying up about another twenty minutes, it's good to have someone just watching the rooms for a few minutes after room check to make sure the kids stay put. If they see you out here, they'll go to bed. If you want to get into bed though, I'll do it."

"We can do it," said Javier.

"Absolutely," agreed Isabela. "Go ahead and go to bed."

Isabela didn't relish spending the next half hour with Javier, but she never would have admitted that to Mr. Jacobs. He looked exhausted. She knew she needed to get past her dislikes and let him go to bed so that he'd be able to function in the morning.

After the band teacher had gone to his own room, Javier turned his attention to Isabela. "I guess we should get started."

"I guess so," said Isabela. "Mr. Jacobs made it seem so easy, but I'll admit, I'm a little nervous."

"Me too," laughed Javier.

The two of them made their way to the first door and knocked on it. When there was no answer, Javier knocked again louder. This time they heard shuffling and whispering on the other side of the door, but still no one answered.

"Do you think the kids are already in bed trying to sleep?" asked Javier. "I hate to wake them if they are."

"No, I heard whispering," said Isabela. "Besides, we have to make sure that all of the girls in this room are really here."

She peered over his shoulder. Kayla, Tamara, Kristin, and Miranda were supposed to be in the room. She remembered Kristin and Miranda, but the faces of the other two girls escaped her.

"Okay, I'll knock again," said Javier. He raised his fist and knocked even louder. Isabela could hear the knock echo throughout the room.

"If that doesn't bring them to the door, nothing will," she commented.

A second later, the door opened. Instead of a teenage girl, a large burly man with a hairy face and chest stared out at them.

"What do you want?" he growled.

"Sorry, wrong room!" said Javier quickly. He grabbed Isabela's arm and led her swiftly down the hall. The door to the hotel room slammed shut behind them.

Javier turned the corner and burst out laughing. "I am so embarrassed!" he exclaimed.

"How did that even happen?" asked Isabela. "Did Mr. Jacobs write down the wrong room number?" She was laughing even harder than Javier.

Javier brought his laughter under control and studied the list. "No," he said sheepishly, "I read the number wrong. It was supposed to be 227. I knocked on 221."

"Well," giggled Isabela, "I'm glad it was you that knocked and not me. That guy looked angry at being woken up."

"I don't think he was sleeping," said Javier.

"Of course, he was sleeping," argued Isabela. "It took him forever to answer the door."

"Yeah," chuckled Javier, "but not because he was asleep."

"Then what was he doing…oh…you don't mean…?" Isabela gasped in a mixture of horror, dismay, and embarrassment.

"Well, I caught a glimpse into the room. Let's just say he wasn't alone in there," replied Javier.

"You mean we interrupted…you think they were…Oh dear!" Isabela burst out laughing. "We had one job. ONE job! And we couldn't even get it right!"

Javier joined in her laughter. "We can never tell anyone about this!"

"It's too funny to keep a secret," chortled Isabela.

"Okay, you can tell people I knocked on the wrong door, but don't tell the kids we interrupted someone doing the wild thing," pleaded Javier between bouts of laughter.

"Deal," giggled Isabela.

"Let's get room checks out of the way," suggested Javier, "only this time, you take the list and make sure I'm knocking on the right rooms."

Isabela took the list and directed him to the first room. Both of them breathed sighs of relief when the door opened, and it was a high school student standing next to the door.

"Room check," said Isabela. "Do you have everyone in your room?

"Yes," replied the boy.

"You have Todd, DeMario, Lance, and Mark?" She glanced up at him after reading the names.

"Yes," repeated the boy. "We're all here."

"Good," said Javier. "Stay in your room and go to bed. It's time for lights out. We'll see you in the morning."

"Okay," replied the boy. He shut the door softly behind him.

"It goes so much better when you have the right room," giggled Isabela.

The rest of the room checks went smoothly. All of the students seemed to have already settled for the night. Even so, Isabela and Javier sat in the lobby for an extra fifteen minutes to make sure that no one tried to sneak out of their room.

"I think we're good to go to our own rooms now," said Javier. He was back in the armchair in front of the gas fireplace.

"I agree," said Isabela. She stood and stretched before heading for her own room. "Don't go into the wrong room," she added over her shoulder. "That will be worse that just knocking on the wrong door."

"Enough!" Javier called after her.

Once inside her room, Isabela changed into a comfortable pair of flannel pajamas and crawled into bed. As she was drifting off to sleep, she realized something that startled her awake. Javier hadn't been annoying during the room checks. Maybe there was hope for the guy after all. She smiled as she snuggled further down under the comforter. Of course, she would never be interested in a guy like him, but at least he was starting to be a little less irritating.

Chapter 7

Morning came much too early for Isabela. When she entered the hotel dining room for breakfast, she was surprised to see how wide awake and alert the kids all seemed. No one would have guessed that it was close to one o'clock when they finally went to bed. Isabela grabbed a muffin and a banana and sat down at one of the corner tables. A few minutes later, Mr. Jacobs joined her.

"As soon as Javier gets here, let's discuss the schedule for today," he said.

Isabela refrained from wrinkling her nose with distaste. Even though Javier hadn't annoyed her during the room checks, it didn't mean she wanted to eat breakfast with him. Still, if the band teacher wanted to talk to both of them at the same time, breakfast was an excellent time to do it.

A moment later, Javier sat down with a large waffle and some bacon on top. "I love these hotel breakfasts," he laughed. "I eat better here than I do at home."

"Now that you're both here," began Mr. Jacobs, "let's talk about how Honor Band works. The coordinators like the students to have a chaperone with them at all times, even during the practice sessions. That way, if a student gets sick or needs something, they have a chaperone there to help. The band teachers usually have different meetings and workshops to attend, so we aren't always available."

"So, what you're saying is we can't go sightseeing," laughed Isabela. "Not that I would even want to in this weather." She pointed toward the window. Snow was beginning to fall.

"That's what I'm saying," grinned Mr. Jacobs. "Anyway, one of you needs to be in the practice room all the time in case there's an issue, which there never is, but just in case."

"Okay," replied Javier. "No problem."

"Good," said Mr. Jacobs. "I'm going to grab an apple, and I'll meet you on the bus."

After Mr. Jacobs was gone, Javier turned to Isabela, "I thought for sure you were going to tattle to him about my poor room-knocking skills."

"To be honest, I'd forgotten all about it," replied Isabela. "Thanks for reminding me that I have a good story to tell."

"What's a good story to tell?" a voice behind Isabela asked.

She turned around to see Alicia and Alejandro standing there. It was Alicia who had spoken.

"Nothing really," said Javier quickly.

"Dad, you're hiding something," said Alejandro. "I can tell. What's the story?"

"Don't worry about it," replied Javier.

"Mom," said Alicia, "what's the story?"

Isabela grinned mischievously. "This is Mr. Varilla's story to tell. Pester him. I'll just say that it's a funny one and leave it at that." Isabela stood and started to walk away from the table, but then she paused and added, "Ask him where he learned to read numbers."

As she exited the dining room, she could hear the two teenagers pelting Javier with questions. She realized that she had set him up, but she couldn't help herself. He could be such an overbearing man sometimes that it gave her great pleasure to put him in his place once in a while.

Thirty minutes later, Isabela was in the practice hall. She found a comfortable chair and pulled out a book from her backpack. She had brought other things to do while the kids practiced, but she was in the mood to read a mystery. Next to her, Javier pulled out his laptop and set it on a table in front of him.

"What are you working on?" asked Isabela curiously.

"It's top secret," replied Javier with a grin. He powered up the computer.

"Funny," said Isabela, "but really, what is it?"

"Really, I can't tell you," said Javier.

Before Isabela could press him again, the Honor Band coordinator moved to the front of the room and asked for everyone's attention. Silence descended on the large hall. It seemed that the students were holding their breath. Isabela had never seen teenagers so still and so quiet.

The program coordinator was a short woman who looked like she would be more at home in a beauty shop than addressing a room full of high school students and their chaperones. However, once she started speaking, Isabela realized that the woman had a large stage presence that more than made up for her diminutive size.

"Welcome, everyone," she began. "We are so excited to have you here for the next couple of days. First, let's do a little housekeeping. Please wear your nametags whenever we are in rehearsal. That will help Dr. Lawrence, our band director, know who you are. Secondly, whenever we have a break, please remember to be back in your seats ready to play five minutes before the break ends. That means that if the break gets over at 1:00, you need to be in your seat ready to go by 12:55. If you sit down at 12:56, you are late. Does everyone understand that?"

Behind her, Isabela heard a chaperone from another school whisper, "Wow! They don't play around here, do they?"

As though the coordinator had heard the comment, she said, "Next, less discuss talking. There shouldn't be any talking or visiting with your neighbor. We are here to learn about music. Chaperones, I'm afraid this applies to you also. We need you to be as quiet as possible so that your students can focus on the music. We just have two short days to put together a wonderful concert."

Isabela glanced surreptitiously over her shoulder. She was just in time to see the speaker behind her blush with embarrassment. Once the coordinator was finished laying out the basic rules, she introduced the director for the Honor Band, and the students began warming up.

Isabela tried to focus on her book, but the constant clacking of the keys on Javier's keyboard distracted her. She was able to tune out the band, but for some reason, Javier kept drawing her attention. She glanced over to see what he was working on. It was some sort of document, but she couldn't make out any of the words.

Once he caught her looking at his screen. Without a word, he tipped the screen just a little so that it was no longer in focus for her.

Her face burned red with both embarrassment and irritation. Why did he care if she knew what he was working on? What did it matter if she saw the front of his screen? Why did he have to be so irritating?

At noon, the director told the kids they could break for lunch. The Richfield kids gathered at the back of the practice room, waiting to be told where they should go to eat. Mr. Jacobs arrived just as the last students stepped up to the group.

"Okay, we have one hour," he reminded the kids.

"Actually, only about fifty minutes," spoke up Alicia. "We have to be in our seats ready to go by 12:55, and some of us have reeds that need to be moistened."

"Good point," said Mr. Jacobs. "We'll plan on having you back here at 12:50. Let's go eat in the Student Union building. They have a cafeteria over there."

Mr. Jacobs led the way outside the building with the group of students following him. Isabela and Javier brought up the rear. Snow blanketed the sidewalks. A slight wind was blowing causing the snow to brush against Isabela's face and down her neck. Involuntarily, she shivered.

"Cold?" asked Javier as he fell in step with her.

"Only when the wind blows snow down my neck," she laughed.

"Rexburg is definitely colder than Richfield," remarked Javier.

"Well, we are about six hours farther north," pointed out Isabela.

Javier didn't bother to answer. He just shrugged his shoulders in agreement. Isabela was about to say more when out of the corner of her eye, she saw a dark shape leaving the sidewalk the group was walking on. Turning, she saw that it was Miranda breaking away from the group.

Isabela hurried forwards in an effort to catch up with the teen. Miranda was walking rapidly. Her black coat was zipped up to her chin, and the hood was pulled down over her forehead. She was walking rapidly into the wind.

"Miranda!" called out Isabela as she hurried after the girl.

The teenager paused and looked behind her. When she saw who it was, she stopped and waited for Isabela to catch up.

"Where are you headed? You're going the wrong direction for the Student Union building," said Isabela as she approached the girl.

"I'm cold and miserable," said Miranda. "I was just going to go in that building over there. She pointed to a nearby building which was labeled as being part of the music department. "I figured I'd just find a vending machine or starve and catch up with the group when they came back."

"It's a good plan," said Isabela sympathetically, "except we want everyone to stick together. The last thing we need is to lose someone here on campus, so cold or not, I'm afraid you're going to have to come with us to the cafeteria."

"All right," said Miranda in resignation. "I'll stick with the group, but I'm going to complain the whole time."

Isabela laughed. "You're a girl after my own heart. In fact, I have a workout shirt that says something like that."

"Do you exercise a lot?" asked Miranda as the pair clomped through the snow back to the sidewalk. "I heard Alicia telling some of the kids on the bus that you're up early everyday so you can go running."

"I exercise almost every day," admitted Isabela. "I enjoy it, and it seems like my day goes better when I get in a good workout."

"That's probably why you look so young," said Miranda. "A lot of the moms look old, but you still look really good for your age."

Isabela raised one eyebrow. She was unsure how to respond to such a left-handed compliment. On the one hand, she'd just been told she looked good; on the other hand, she'd also been informed that she was old.

"Thanks, I think," she said with a laugh.

"Do you even know where we're going?" asked Miranda suddenly.

"Not really," admitted Isabela. "I'm following the tracks on the sidewalk and hoping they'll lead us to the right building, but if we don't hurry, we won't even have tracks to follow. I think the snow's coming down harder."

"I think you're right," said Miranda with a shiver. "I hate winter."

"What do you miss most about Phoenix," asked Isabela curiously.

"Well, right now, it's warm weather," laughed Miranda, but then she instantly sobered. "I miss everything about it. I really don't like Richfield that much."

"Maybe if you gave it an honest chance, you'd like it," suggested Isabela. Her heart went out to Miranda. It must have been hard to be forced to move at the beginning of her junior year of high school.

"I kind of did when I first got here," said Miranda, "but not really. I just didn't want to be here, and Aunt Zoe was acting weird, and well…you know."

No, Isabela didn't know, but she could tell she wasn't going to get any other information out of Miranda at the moment. She noticed that the tracks they were following turned right onto a different sidewalk which ended at a building with a sign identifying itself as the Student Union.

"This is our destination," said Isabela, pointing at the structure.

"Thank goodness!" announced Miranda. "I'm freezing."

Isabela hurried forward and opened the door so that Miranda could enter without taking her hands out of her pockets. Miranda smiled in gratitude and hurried forward towards the cafeteria which was just inside the doors.

Isabela pulled off her cap and gloves and stuffed them into a pocket of her coat. She went into the cafeteria and grabbed a tray. She noticed a soup and salad bar and hurried over to it. A cup of hot soup would do wonders towards warming her up.

Out of the corner of her eye, she saw Miranda join a group of girls. At least, the youth had someone to hang out with and wouldn't be forced to eat lunch alone.

Once Isabela had her soup and salad, she surveyed the area, looking for a place to sit. The cafeteria was crowded with college students and high school band students. Off in the corner, she saw Javier and Mr. Jacobs sitting at a small table. Javier caught her eye and signaled her over.

"Where did you go?" asked Javier as she sat down at the table. "One second you were next to me, and then suddenly you were gone."

"We almost lost a student," said Isabela. "I was herding her back with the rest of the group."

"Who did we lose?" asked Mr. Jacobs in concern.

"Miranda. She broke off from the group," Isabela replied.

"Why would she do that?" asked Mr. Jacobs. His eyes squinted with worry.

"She said that she was cold and miserable. She was just going to go into a nearby building and hope they had a vending machine. If they didn't, she planned on starving. She was going to just wait until we went past and rejoin us," explained Isabela. "I told her she had to stay with the group."

"I'm glad you caught her," said Mr. Jacobs. "She needs to hang out with the group. She's had a rough life lately, and this trip could really help her get some good friends."

"I was wondering what her story is," remarked Isabela, "but I didn't want to pry or be nosy."

"Which one is Miranda?" spoke up Javier.

"She's the girl with the dark black hair that is obviously dyed and the eyebrow piercing," replied Mr. Jacobs.

"So, what's going on with her?" asked Javier, "unless of course, you can't tell us."

"I don't know a lot," admitted Mr. Jacobs, "but I can tell you what is common knowledge. I won't say anything that's too personal, but it might help you two as chaperones if you have a little insight into her history."

Isabela took a bite of her soup as she listened. It was a creamy potato and cheese and was delicious. She didn't know if it was because she was cold and hungry or if this cafeteria had a secret recipe, but the soup was one of the best she had ever tasted.

"I'd appreciate knowing more about her if it will help her," said Isabela after she swallowed the spoonful of soup. "She told me that she moved here from Phoenix because of family problems, and she is homesick."

"I'd be homesick too if I left all that good sunshine for this cold weather," said Javier.

"Wow," said Mr. Jacobs. "She really downplayed her story. She moved here because her mother died in a car accident."

"Oh, no!" gasped Isabela. "I had no idea. I just assumed it was something like a divorce."

Mr. Jacobs took a deep breath. "Her mom was dating a guy that Miranda didn't get along with. He was driving drunk when the accident occurred. Miranda's mom died in the car crash, and the boyfriend almost died. He's in jail now. Miranda was with them, but she managed to walk away with just a few cuts and bruises. Miranda's mom and her sister were twins: Zoe and Chloe. The aunt took Miranda in. It's been a rocky transition for both of them. Zoe suddenly has a daughter, and she lost her twin sister. Miranda had to move, she lost her mom, and she survived a horrible car crash."

"Oh, my goodness!" exclaimed Isabela. "I work with Miranda's aunt. No wonder she's been so grumpy the past few months. I had no idea she was going through all of that. Now I feel bad for some of the unkind things I said about her."

"Well, now you know the story about Miranda. She's an amazing flutist. I hope this trip helps her adjust to Richfield High School a little better," said Mr. Jacobs.

At that moment, a tall heavyset man with dark hair and a mustache approached the table. He was carrying a tray with a large serving of lasagna on it. "Hey, Les, mind if I join you?" He indicated the empty chair between Javier and Mr. Jacobs.

"Please do," said Mr. Jacobs. "This is Tim Dahl. He's the band teacher from South Sevier High School."

"Aren't they our rivals?" asked Javier. He scooted his chair closer to Isabela to accommodate Mr. Dahl.

"Only on the sports field," laughed Mr. Dahl. "Les and I actually went to college together. We were even roommates for a semester."

"Why not longer?" asked Isabela. She didn't really care, but Javier was sitting ridiculously close to her. She could almost feel charges of electricity going between them. She didn't know what that meant, but she was acutely aware of his presence next to her.

"Les decided to go and get married on me," replied Mr. Dahl. "I guess he liked Anna's company better than mine. I'll never understand that."

Everyone around the table laughed at the comment, and the two teachers began trading stories of their college days, trying to convince Isabela and Javier that the other one had been the negative influence in the friendship.

During the banter, Mr. Jacobs glanced at his watch. "We need to be back in about fifteen minutes. I'm going to start gathering kids. I'll meet you guys by the front doors."

"I need to get my kids gathered up too," said Mr. Dahl, standing. "It was nice meeting you two."

"So how do you like chaperoning?" asked Javier after the teachers left. He shifted his chair over a few inches so that he was no longer sitting so close to Isabela. For some reason, she missed the closeness of his body.

"It's okay," replied Isabela, trying to ignore the sense of loss she was feeling. "A little boring at times. I'm glad I brought something to read. What are you working on so busily with your laptop?"

"I told you, it's top secret," grinned Javier.

"That joke wasn't funny the first time you told it. Now it's just annoying. If you don't want to tell me, just say it's none of my business," replied Isabela.

"Okay, it's none of your business," said Javier. This time the smile was absent from his face.

"You are so rude," said Isabela, standing up from the table.

"But you said…" Javier's face was a mixture of confusion and astonishment.

"I didn't mean literally," said Isabela. "Obviously, it's none of my business. I was just trying to make conversation."

Before Javier could say anything else, Isabela stomped off to empty her tray. She knew she was overreacting, but she didn't know how to handle the embarrassment she felt at being put in her place by this man.

The walk back to the practice hall was made in silence. Once or twice, Javier cleared his throat like he was about to say something, but Isabela quickened her steps so she wouldn't have to walk next to him. Ahead of her, she saw Miranda walking and laughing with some of the other kids from the band. Like Mr. Jacobs, she hoped that Miranda would adjust to living in Richfield.

Back in the practice hall, Javier pulled out a thick book rather than his laptop and began to read. He had his feet propped comfortably on the chair in front of him.

Isabela tried to concentrate on her own book, but she had a difficult time focusing. For some reason, she missed the constant clacking of the keys on Javier's laptop. It was almost as though she missed being constantly reminded that he was next to her, but of course, that was ridiculous, so she quickly pushed that idea from her mind.

Chapter 8

When practice ended for the day, Mr. Jacobs announced that they were going to a bowling alley on the other end of town. The kids chattered excitedly at the prospect of going bowling. Isabela smiled as she saw groups being formed and challenges being issued. By the time they arrived at the bowling alley, it seemed that everyone had a group to bowl with.

Isabela went to a bench and sat down where she could watch the kids bowl. She noticed that Mr. Jacobs was sitting with a group of boys who had apparently been challenged by a group of girls. She wondered if Mr. Jacobs was any good at bowling. Considering the number of band trips he took the kids on, she guessed that he probably could hold his own against the kids.

Javier came up and sat down next to Isabela. "Why aren't you out there bowling?"

"They don't have any alleys with bumper pads set up," she joked.

"I'll ask them to set some up if you'll bowl a game with me," said Javier with a grin.

"And have all the band kids make fun of me for the rest of the trip?" she asked.

"Seriously, though," said Javier, "I'm not like Mr. Jacobs. I don't really want to bowl with the kids. Come and bowl a game with me."

"I'm horrible," protested Isabela. "I won't be any competition at all."

"I'm not very good either," said Javier, "but I'll tell you what, if I get too far ahead, I'll switch and bowl with my left hand."

"I'm holding you to that," laughed Isabela as she stood up and headed for the desk, so they could rent shoes and buy a game.

It turned out that Isabela and Javier were evenly matched, with each throwing their share of gutter balls. Isabela managed to get a strike, but Javier got two spares. As they bowled, they bantered back and forth about what sort of pay-off the loser should do for the winner. Isabela was holding out for ice cream, but Javier wanted the loser to buy dinner.

"You know what," laughed Isabela when she managed to get a second strike, "I don't know why I'm worried about the cost of this little wager we have going on here. I can afford to have you pay for dinner, so dinner it is."

"Now just a minute," protested Javier as he watched Isabela's score creep into first place. "Ice cream is actually sounding better the more I think of it."

"Either way, I win," laughed Isabela. Javier had just thrown his third gutter ball. Even if he knocked over all of the pins on his next try, Isabela would still be the winner.

"Growl," laughed Javier as he retrieved his ball.

He tossed it towards the pins. It truly was a toss. The ball bounced twice before moving shakily down the lane and knocking over four pins. Isabela was officially the winner.

"Ice cream," she announced as she did a little victory dance. "I want ice cream."

"Fine. I'll buy you ice cream," sighed Javier. "Good game though."

Isabela sat down on the bench and began untying her shoes. "It was fun. I haven't bowled in years. I'd forgotten how much I enjoyed it."

"You know," said Javier, sitting down next to her on the bench, "we kind of got off to a rocky start that day we met in the parking lot. I'm sorry for splashing water all over you and then yelling at you. You scared me. I turned the corner and suddenly you were in front of me. I thought I was going to hit you."

"I thought you were going to hit me too," said Isabela. "That's why I yelled at you. I had a major adrenalin rush when you came barreling at me. You really were going too fast for the conditions."

"I was not..." Javier started to protest, but then he softened. "Yes, I probably was. I was in a hurry that day. Even so, you should watch where you're going. What if I hadn't noticed you?"

"Actually, I was watching," said Isabela. She was feeling mildly defensive. "As I was coming down the sidewalk from the high school, I looked. No one was coming. Then just as I got to the curb, the wind blew my hair in my face. I thought I could see good enough to make a final check, but apparently, I couldn't."

"So...we both could have done things a little differently," said Javier softly.

"Yes, I guess we could have," Isabela agreed reluctantly. She really wanted to place all the blame on Javier, but she knew that she could have been more careful as well.

"So...you'll forgive me for the parking lot?" asked Javier.

"Yes, if you'll forgive me," replied Isabela.

"Done," said Javier with a smile. "Let's go get our real shoes."

Isabela followed him to the counter and retrieved her boots. She quickly slipped them on her feet, reveling in the warmth the boots provided. Next to her, Javier was slipping on a pair of sturdy hiking boots.

Isabela surveyed the groups of kids. Most of them were starting a second game. She noticed that Miranda had wandered away from her group and was sitting by herself at the snack bar. The girl looked lonely and sad.

"I'm going to go over and talk to Miranda," she told Javier, indicating where the girl was sitting with a nod of her head.

"Okay, I'll go see what the other kids are up to," he replied.

As she stepped toward Miranda, Javier suddenly took her arm with a surprising gentleness and stopped her. She looked up at him in surprise. He had a serious look on his face.

"Thanks for the game, Isa," he said to her. "It was fun."

Before she could reply, he walked away in the direction of the bowlers. Her arm was still warm where he had touched her. Inside she felt a small burst of happiness. She'd never been called Isa before, always Isabela, but she found that she quite liked the nickname when Javier said it.

Chapter 9

Isabela made her way over to Miranda. The girl was busy on her phone and didn't see Isabela until she slid into a chair across the table from Miranda.

"Did you get tired of bowling?" asked Isabela.

"A little bit," said Miranda. "I bowled a game, but it just wasn't as fun as I thought it would be." She hesitated a moment before adding, "I'm not very good. It's hard to get excited when you're losing so bad that there's no hope of ever catching up."

"I can relate to that," replied Isabela. "I'm pretty bad too. Luckily, Mr. Varilla isn't much better."

Miranda chuckled slightly at the comment but didn't reply. Isabela glanced around the bowling alley. Most of the kids were still bowling, although several had gotten food and were eating it while they bowled.

"I think I'm going to have some fries," announced Isabela. "If I get them will you share them with me?"

"No, thanks," replied Miranda. "I'm not really hungry."

"I'm not either," Isabela confessed. "But I'm craving fries. Will you help me eat them, so I don't make a pig of myself?"

"I guess so," Miranda shrugged.

Isabela hurried over to the snack counter and asked for an order of fries. She sensed that Miranda might benefit from talking to someone, and Isabela had learned through parenting Alicia and her years working as a nurse that nothing seems to help a person open up quite as well as a shared snack.

Isabela placed the fries on the table between them. She took one and popped it in her mouth. Miranda finished the text she was composing before she turned her attention to the fries.

"How are you liking Honor Band?" asked Isabela in an effort to get the conversation started.

"I like it," said Miranda. "We never did Honor Band in Phoenix. I'm sure they had it, but my teacher wasn't big on trips. He focused on concerts."

"Well, I'm glad you got to come on this trip," said Isabela.

"I am too," Miranda replied.

Miranda's phone dinged and she picked it up to read the text. Isabela watched as her fingers flew across the keyboard in reply. Isabela was always impressed at how effortless teens made texting seem. If Isabela didn't pay attention or if she went too fast, her texts were filled with mistakes.

"Are you texting one of your old friends back in Phoenix?" asked Isabela curiously.

"Sort of, but not really. I'm texting my best friend from Phoenix. She's a couple years older than me though, so she already graduated. She went to college, so she's not in Phoenix anymore," replied Miranda.

"Where did she go to college?" Isabela took another fry and popped it into her mouth. Across the room, she saw Javier watching Alicia and Alejandro play. He had a quiet attractiveness about him that made her heart flutter. She quickly turned her attention back to Miranda.

"Iduh…know for sure," mumbled Miranda.

"What?" asked Isabela.

"I don't know for sure…I don't really remember," Miranda confessed.

"You don't remember?" Isabella was confused.

Knowing where your best friend moved for college seemed like such a basic thing to know, but maybe kids were different these days.

"She had a few colleges lined up. I can't remember which one she chose, and I had a lot of family stuff going on at the time," explained Miranda.

"Oh, that makes sense," said Isabela. She wanted to ask more, but she could tell that the conversation had moved into forbidden territory.

"What's your friend's name?" Isabela figured talking about the friend would be more acceptable that discussing Miranda's family troubles.

"Caitlin," replied Miranda. "We've been friends since middle school."

"Were you neighbors?" asked Isabela. "It's unusual for best friends to be two years apart in age."

"Actually, we met in an art class. We ended up sitting by each other because we have the same last name. We just sort of clicked. We used to tell people that I was her little sister, and they believed us. Even a lot of the teachers thought we were sisters," Miranda laughed at the memory.

"That's so much fun!" Isabela joined in the girl's laughter. "My best friend and I used to try to convince people that we were twins."

"How did that work out for you?" asked Miranda.

"Not very well," Isabela admitted. "My best friend was tall and blonde. She looked like a Barbie doll."

Miranda laughed at the idea of Isabela and a blonde girl trying to convince people that they were twins. "Why did you even think that would work?" Miranda asked.

"We were in middle school. It made sense at the time," Isabela said with a shrug.

At that moment, Alicia and Alejandro approached the table. "We're leaving," said Alicia.

Isabela glanced around. Many of the students had already exited the bowling alley. Others were busily putting on coats and hats before heading outside.

"Nice talk," said Isabela with a smile.

"Thanks for the fries," replied Miranda.

"I'm glad you were willing to help me eat them," answered Isabela as she pulled on her heavy parka. Miranda smiled in reply. Isabela couldn't help but notice that when she smiled, Miranda's entire countenance lit up.

When Isabela stepped outside the bowling alley, a full-blown snowball fight was in progress. It seemed that several of the students had ganged up against Mr. Jacobs and Javier. A few students had come to the adults' side and were busily trying to help the men in the onslaught of snowballs they were facing.

Isabela laughed as a snowball hit Javier on top of his head, knocking his beanie off. She turned to see who the thrower was. It was Alejandro, fighting against his own father.

The air was filled with snowballs. Isabela stood near the door of the bowling alley so that she wouldn't get caught by a stray missile. At first, it seemed that Mr. Jacob's side was losing, but gradually, they began to gain ground against the students attacking them. Several girls were crouched in the snow making snowballs as fast as they could for Javier, Mr. Jacobs, and four boys. The adults and the teens who were throwing put the snowballs to good use. The other group didn't seem to be as well-organized. Their plan was a simple one: grab snow, make a ball, attack. Unfortunately, the strategy wasn't efficient, and before long, Mr. Jacobs had reached the door of the bus.

"All right!" he called. "That's it. We win."

In response, one more snowball flew through the air, landing harmlessly on the ground next to him. He looked at the snowball and then back at the kids. His face plainly said that it was time to cease fire.

"Let's load up and head back to the hotel. If we go now, you'll have time to go swimming if you want to," he announced.

The idea of swimming seemed to appeal to the teenagers, even though the ground was covered with over a foot of snow and more was threatening to fall. With flushed faces, they surged quickly to the bus, so they could get back to the hotel.

Isabela crossed the parking lot. Just before she reached the bus, a large, wet snowball smashed into her face. Gasping, she brushed away the snow and looked around to see who had thrown it. Javier was standing several feet away with a large grin on his face.

"Gotcha!" he laughed.

"Why did you do that?" she spluttered. "That was cold, and now I'm cold and wet! Did you have to hit me in the face."

"Sorry," he said contritely. "I didn't mean to get you in the face…but you have to admit, it was kind of funny."

"I'll admit nothing of the sort. It wasn't funny," said Isabela hotly.

She turned and climbed onto the bus. When she got to her seat, she turned and stared out the window so she wouldn't have to look at Javier when he entered the bus. She was furious with him for throwing the snowball. He had no right to do that. She wasn't part of their snowball fight.

She heard him sit in his seat across the aisle. She stole a quick glance at him. The smile was gone from his face. He looked despondent, like a little kid who has gotten in trouble and is waiting to find out what his punishment will be.

She turned her attention back to the window. She was overreacting. She knew she was being ridiculous, and that knowledge just made her angrier.

She didn't even know why she was so upset with Javier or why she was angry with herself for being irritated. For just a moment, she wondered if it was because she was starting to fall for him, but she quickly pushed the thought from her consciousness. No. She was upset because he was an overbearing jerk. It had nothing to do with the idea that she might be developing feelings for him. That was definitely not the case.

Chapter 10

When they reached the hotel, there was a mad dash of kids hurrying to get off the bus, so they could go swimming in the hotel pool. Isabela made her way down the aisle of the bus. She was painfully aware of Javier right behind her. Mr. Jacobs stopped her before she could get off the bus.

"Do you two mind going and monitoring the kids at the pool for a few minutes?" he asked. "I have some phone calls that I need to make before I can go down with them."

"Sure, no problem," spoke Javier before Isabela could answer.

Isabela wanted to snap, "Speak for yourself," but she bit her tongue. She knew that she would have responded the same way if Javier hadn't spoken up first.

Besides, maybe he was speaking just for himself. She didn't have to join him at the pool. She could say that she had a headache or just didn't feel well.

No one would fault her for skipping the pool, but she knew that the safety of the kids was first, and even if she'd had a headache, she would have gone to the pool with the kids anyway.

The pool was a madhouse when Isabela entered. She had changed into her bathing suit, but she had no intention of going swimming. She just didn't want her street clothes to get wet. She had her long hair piled on top of her head in a messy bun. She knew that the look was a good one on her because it brought out her dark eyes.

Her plan had been to sit on the opposite side of the pool from Javier. Unfortunately, when she entered the pool area, she saw that all the chairs were grouped together along one side of the pool, and most of the empty chairs were already taken by teenagers. The only available place to sit was right next to Javier.

Isabela sat down tentatively next to him. He was wearing a t-shirt and swim trunks. Isabela could see his muscles beneath the thin fabric of his shirt. The expression on his face seemed pensive. She could tell that he possessed both a mental and a physical strength that she had been unaware of before.

The students were splashing around in the pool, playing a game that seemed to be a mix of Marco Polo, Shark, and Tag. The kids screamed with laughter as they played.

"They'll sleep good tonight," commented Javier.

His voice was quiet and formal. The easygoing feelings they'd had between them earlier were completely gone. Isabela knew that it was mostly her fault. She had overreacted in the parking lot. Logically, she knew that Javier hadn't meant to hit her in the face. He wasn't the type of guy to do something that might hurt another person.

The two sat in silence for several minutes, watching the kids play. Water was splashing everywhere. Isabela was glad she hadn't tried to wear regular clothes. The silence between her and Javier stretched out uncomfortably. Isabela knew she needed to apologize, but she really hated to admit that she was wrong, especially to Javier.

Finally, she took a deep breath and cleared her throat. "I'm sorry for back there…in the parking lot, I mean."

Javier looked over at her and raised one eyebrow. He didn't respond. He just sat and stared at her. Obviously, he wasn't going to make this easy for her.

"I'm sorry I yelled at you. I overreacted," she continued.

"Ya think?" he replied.

"Look, I'm trying to apologize," she said hotly. "If you don't want to accept the apology, just say so. I'm not going to get down on my knees and grovel."

"It's fine," he said after a long pause. "I get it. We had a long day. You were tired. You're female."

"I'm female? What's that supposed to mean?" demanded Isabela.

"Just that you're temperamental. Women get their feelings hurt easily," he replied.

"It's not about getting my feelings hurt. You threw a snowball in my face. In my face! You don't throw things at women's faces. We don't like it," Isabela said angrily.

"Because it ruins your makeup?" he asked.

"Because it's rude!" Isabela stood up abruptly. She walked away from him and exited the pool. He could watch the kids by himself for a bit. Then after she had calmed down, she would go back and take a turn.

As she started down the hallway, she ran into Mr. Jacobs. He was wearing a pair of navy swim trunks. He was carrying two small children's tubes on his arm. He grinned when he saw her.

"I'm about to become the life of the party. The kids will love these floaties," he said enthusiastically. "Are you leaving?"

"Yes, I thought I'd call it an evening, but I can stay if you need me to. Javier is still down there," she replied.

"No, go ahead. Meet in the lobby at ten for room checks," replied Mr. Jacobs.

Isabela agreed, but she dreaded doing the room checks with Javier. Things had been good between them earlier, but now she was angry with him again. *Why were men so stupid? She wondered. Why did they have to ruin so many good things?*

For a moment, she was taken back to when she was married to Alicia's father. That had been many years ago. Adan had been rude, judgmental, and overbearing, and those were his good points. When he'd been drinking, which was often, he was downright mean. It was the meanness that ended the marriage. Isabela could put up with a lot of things, but not when someone was purposely unkind.

As she reflected on her previous marriage, she wondered if that was part of the reason why she had overreacted with Javier. Was she trying to protect herself from getting hurt again? Was she afraid to trust that there might be a nice guy out there?

Of course, that line of thinking was ridiculous. She wasn't interested in remarriage or even a relationship. And she certainly wasn't interested in Javier. But if she wasn't interested in him, why did she feel so empty now that things weren't good between them?

Upon returning to her room, Isabela changed out of her swimsuit into a pair of comfortable leggings and oversized shirt. She leaned back on the bed and surfed channels on the television, looking for something to watch. She finally decided on a sitcom.

She was just getting into the episode when her phone chimed, signaling that she had a text. She was surprised to see that the message was from Javier.

I'm sorry ☹ Forgive me?

She paused a moment before typing out her reply. *Only if you forgive me for overreacting.*

Her phone chimed again. *Deal! See ya at 10 for room checks.*

Isabela set her phone on the bed next to her. Suddenly, she was looking forward to ten o'clock.

Chapter 11

A few minutes before ten, Isabela met Javier and Mr. Jacobs in the lobby. "Are you ready?" asked Mr. Jacobs.

"You can go ahead and get to bed if you want," said Javier. "We're pros at it now. Last night went off without a hitch."

Isabela burst out laughing. "Well, almost, but we did manage to make sure *everyone* was in their room." She laughed even harder as she emphasized the word everyone.

"Really?" said Javier good-naturedly. "I thought we agreed we'd never discuss that."

"Discuss what? What happened?" asked Mr. Jacobs. His face was a picture of confusion. Isabela could tell that he wasn't sure if he should be worried or amused.

"Nothing," replied Isabela innocently. "Javier is just really thorough at this job."

"Thorough?" questioned Mr. Jacobs.

"Oh fine!" laughed Javier. "I'll confess. One of the doors I knocked on last night didn't belong to anyone in our group!"

"I've made that mistake before," chuckled Mr. Jacobs. "Did anyone answer the door?"

"Oh, yes, and he was not happy." Javier shook his head at the memory.

"Because you woke him up?" asked Mr. Jacobs.

"Worse," said Javier.

"Worse? What could be worse?" asked Mr. Jacobs. "Unless…oh, no! How embarrassing!"

"You have no idea! Especially at breakfast this morning," agreed Javier.

"Wait! You saw him at breakfast this morning?" asked Isabela.

"Yep! I ran right into him next to the coffee. Suddenly, I wasn't feeling hungry anymore," laughed Javier.

"Do you think he recognized you?" asked Mr. Jacobs.

"The way he glared at me," said Javier, "I'm going to say yes, he recognized me."

"Well, that's awkward," laughed Mr. Jacobs.

"So now you know my secret," chuckled Javier. "I'm a very thorough chaperone. I make sure the entire hotel is in bed."

"Well, I can't argue with that kind of attention to detail," said Mr. Jacobs. "If you two don't mind doing the room checks, then I'll head to bed."

"We don't mind at all," said Isabela.

After Mr. Jacobs was gone, Javier handed Isabela the list of rooms. "Make sure I only knock on the right doors," he told her with a smile.

As Isabela took the list from Javier, her fingers accidentally brushed against his. Her skin tingled with the contact. She glanced up at his face to see if he had felt the same electricity, but his face remained impassive.

"Let's start with the boys' rooms," she suggested quickly. For some reason, she felt her face redden. She turned and headed down the hall before Javier noticed that she was blushing.

Even though it was only a little after ten, all of the boys were already settled for the night. Apparently, the early morning and the full day of activities had completely worn the boys out. Once the boys' rooms were finished, the pair began knocking on the girls' rooms. The first room was the one Miranda was staying in. Isabela hoped Miranda would answer the door so that she could talk to her just a little more. She felt like she and the teen were beginning to connect. Instead, Kayla, one of the senior girls, opened the door.

"Time for room checks," said Isabela cheerfully. "Do you have everyone in your room?"

"Yep, we're all here," said Kayla.

"Do you have Kayla, Miranda, Kristin, and Tamara?" asked Javier, consulting the list.

"Everyone except Miranda," said Kayla.

"I thought you said everyone is in your room," spoke up Isabela.

"They are. Miranda traded rooms," replied Kayla.

"What do you mean, Miranda traded rooms? When did she do this? Did she get permission from Mr. Jacobs? Who did she trade with?" Javier peppered the girl with questions.

"She just did it today. I assume she asked Mr. Jacobs, but I don't really know. And she didn't trade with anyone. One of the other rooms only had three people, and she decided she wanted to stay with them tonight." Kayla shrugged to show that Miranda's behavior was out of her control.

"Whose room did she move to?" asked Isabela.

"She's in with Jenna, Lainey, and Maria," replied Kayla.

"Thanks," said Isabela. "It's time for bed, so stay in your room and go to sleep. Remember, we're checking out in the morning, so you have to have all your stuff in the parking lot ready to load up by 8:15."

"Okay, we'll be ready," said Kayla as she closed the door softly behind her.

"I wonder if Miranda really did ask Mr. Jacobs if she could switch rooms," said Javier as they made their way to the next room.

"I seriously doubt it," laughed Isabela. "She probably didn't think it mattered."

The next two rooms were checked without incident. When they knocked on Alicia's door, Isabela could tell that the girls in her room were already in bed and falling asleep. Isabela apologized for disturbing the girls.

"It's okay, Mom," said Alicia with a big yawn. "We knew you were coming. I waited up for you. Night."

The final room on the list was the one Miranda had moved to. "I'm a little surprised Miranda wanted to be in this room," remarked Isabela as Javier tapped gently on the door. "The girls in this room are younger than she is."

The girl who opened the door was a freshman, but with her petite frame, she could have passed as a seventh grader. "What's up?" she asked. Behind her, Isabela could hear girls laughing and giggling.

"It sounds like you have all the girls from our school in there," commented Isabela.

"Are we being too loud?" The freshman girl's eyes widened with horror at the idea that she might get in trouble on a school trip.

"Maybe just a little," remarked Isabela. "We're doing room checks. It's time for bed. Remember, we're checking out tomorrow, so you need to have all your stuff packed up and at the bus by 8:15."

"Okay, we'll be ready," said the girl. "And we'll try to be quieter."

"Try to go to sleep," suggested Javier. "Do you have everyone in your room?"

"Yep, all three of us are here," said the freshman.

"What? Three of you?" spoke up Isabela. "You're supposed to have four."

"No, only three were assigned to our room," said the little girl.

"You should have Jenna, Lainey, Maria, and Miranda," said Isabela reading off the list.

"Not Miranda," the girl corrected. "She's a junior, so she's staying in a room with older girls."

"We were told by her roommates that she switched to this room," said Javier.

"That's the first I've heard of it," said the girl. "She's not here. You can come in and see."

By now, the other two girls in the room had come to the door. They'd overheard the conversation and wanted to know what was going on.

"Have any of you seen Miranda?" asked Javier.

"Not since we went bowling," replied one of the other girls. She was tall and thin with braces. In another year, she would be model-beautiful, but at the moment she was still in her awkward stage.

The other two girls nodded their heads in agreement. None of them had seen Miranda since the bowling alley.

"Go ahead and go to bed," Isabela instructed in a no-nonsense voice. "Don't come out of your room."

The girls' eyes widened, and they quickly closed the door. Isabela had the feeling that they were afraid they were in trouble for losing Miranda.

"What now?" she asked after the girls were back in their room.

"Let's go back to the room Miranda's supposed to be in and see if she came back," suggested Javier.

The two made their way back down the hallway to Miranda's room. Javier tapped on the door with sharp, staccato knocks. A few seconds later, Kayla opened the door again.

"Did Miranda come back to this room?" asked Javier.

"No, why would she?" replied Kayla.

"She's not in the room you said she moved to. Those girls didn't even know Miranda was thinking about moving," answered Javier.

"Maybe I got the room wrong," suggested Kayla. "I thought that's the room she said, but maybe she said a different room."

"Okay, thanks," said Javier as Kayla closed the door.

"I guess we need to check the other girls' rooms," said Isabela.

"I think we should check the boys' rooms also," said Javier. "We never asked if any of the rooms had extra kids except for the room that Miranda supposedly moved to."

"Good idea," replied Isabela. "Let's divide the list, so we can get done more quickly. You do the boys. I'll do the girls." Before Javier could protest, Isabela ripped the list in half. She handed the top portion of the room assignments to Javier.

The two separated and quickly made their way through the rest of the rooms, searching for Miranda. Ten minutes later, they met back in the lobby. Neither one of them had located the teen.

"Now what?" asked Javier.

"Let's go back to the room she's supposed to be in and see if her luggage is there," suggested Isabela. "If it is, then we know she's probably coming back."

Javier nodded his head in agreement and followed Isabela down the hall to the room. He knocked on the door a third time.

"What now?" asked Kayla. Her good mood was starting to evaporate. "You expect us to go to bed early, but then you won't let us sleep?"

"We can't find Miranda," spoke up Isabela.

"Oh my gosh!" said Kayla. "Do you think she's hurt or kidnapped?"

"I hope not!" exclaimed Isabela. "I didn't even think about her being kidnapped. When was the last time you saw her?"

"At the bowling alley," Kayla replied promptly. "I haven't seen her since we got back to the hotel."

"What about her stuff?" asked Javier. "Did she leave any of her luggage behind?"

Kayla shook her head. "No, she packed everything in a backpack, and her backpack's gone. That's one of the reasons that we assumed she switched rooms like she told us."

"Do you by any chance have her phone number?" asked Isabela.

"Actually, I do," replied Kayla. "Hang on."

She disappeared into the room. A few seconds later she was back in the doorway with her cell phone. She scrolled through her contact list until she came to Miranda's name. "Here it is." She quickly read off the number while Isabela entered it into her own phone.

"Thanks," said Isabela. "One last question. Since Miranda didn't switch rooms, do you have any idea where she might have gone?"

"No idea," replied Kayla. "When we were with her, she seemed fine. I have no idea where she might have gone."

Javier thanked Kayla, and she shut the door again. He and Isabela looked at each other helplessly.

"What now?" asked Javier.

"Let me try calling her," suggested Isabela. "She might just be getting a shake or a burger at one of the restaurants."

Javier nodded his assent as Isabela pulled up Miranda's number. The call went straight to voicemail. Miranda tried again. Still no luck. This time Isabela left a message.

"I'm going to text her," she told Javier.

Miranda, this is Ms. San Pedro. We have been looking for you. Where are you? Please contact me ASAP so that I know you're safe. Once the message was composed, she hit send.

"What now?" she asked Javier. "Her phone is probably off, so who knows when she'll get my message."

"We need to call Mr. Jacobs and tell him that we're missing a kid," said Javier.

"Great!" said Isabela. "And to think that last night our biggest worry was knocking on the wrong door. Tonight, we have to tell him we lost one of his kids."

"Let's go," said Javier.

"I'm so worried about her," said Isabela. The words caught in her throat as she spoke.

Javier paused and wrapped his arms around Isabela. She leaned into him, drawing comfort from his strong presence.

"I know you are," he whispered in her ear.

They moved swiftly down the hallway to Mr. Jacobs's room. They needed to find Miranda before something horrible happened to her.

Chapter 12

"What do you mean, Miranda's missing?" asked Mr. Jacobs after the pair knocked on his door to tell him what was happening.

The teacher was dressed in flannel pajama pants and an oversized t-shirt that said: "Band Teachers Rock". His hair was disheveled, and it was obvious to both Isabela and Javier that they had woken him with their news.

"Maybe she's just in another room," suggested Mr. Jacobs.

"She's not," said Javier. "We already thought of that."

He proceeded to tell Mr. Jacobs everything they had done to try to locate the missing teen, including calling and texting her phone. When they ran out of ideas, they decided it was time to notify the band teacher.

Mr. Jacobs ran a hand through his hair making it stand up even more. He sighed deeply with anxiety.

"This is serious," said Mr. Jacobs. "I've never lost a kid before on a trip. I'm not even sure what my next step should be. You guys have already done everything I would do. Usually when a kid goes missing, they're with someone else, and they just took off for a store or a late-night snack. The fact that her stuff is missing makes this all the more worrisome."

"We were thinking about gathering all the kids and asking them if Miranda said anything to any of them. Maybe she said something that would give us a clue as to where she is," said Isabela.

"But we didn't do it because most of the kids are asleep by now," added Javier.

"It's a good place to start," agreed Mr. Jacobs as he ran his fingers through his hair, messing it up even more.

"What if we just called each room, rather than have all the band kids gather together?" suggested Javier. "That way, if they don't know anything, they can go back to bed."

"Excellent idea," said Mr. Jacobs.

"And we can divide up the rooms," said Isabela. "We'll get done faster that way."

"Let's do that," agreed Mr. Jacobs.

The band teacher stepped back into his room and got his list of kids. He quickly divided the list into three sections.

The trio decided to go to their own rooms and call the hotel phone in each room since they didn't have everyone's cell phone number. Once they had finished calling their assigned rooms, they would meet back in the lobby.

The first room on Isabela's list was Alicia's. When she called the room, Janie, one of Alicia's friends, answered the phone. Her voice was husky with sleep.

"Hey, Janie," said Isabela. "I need you to wake everyone in your room and ask them a question. Miranda is missing. I need you to ask if Miranda said anything to any of them that might give us a clue as to where she went."

"What?" asked Janie in confusion.

Isabela instantly realized that this was going to be harder than she expected. The kids were asleep and not functioning. It would be hard to get a straight answer out of any of them over the phone.

"Wake your roommates. Tell them that I'm coming over to speak to them. Once I've talked to all of you, you can go back to bed," she told the teen.

Before leaving her room, Isabela called the other rooms on her list and told them that she would be coming to visit and to make sure everyone was awake. As she walked toward the first room, she texted Mr. Jacobs and Javier to tell them what she was doing in case they had run into similar problems of incoherent teenagers.

A moment later, she saw Mr. Jacobs and Javier step outside their rooms. "Great idea," said Javier. "My first kid kept falling asleep on the phone."

Isabela knocked on Alicia's door. Janie answered her knock and invited her inside. The other three girls in the room were in bed. Alicia had a pillow over her face to block out the light Janie had turned on. Samantha groaned when Isabela started speaking.

"I'm sorry to wake you girls," she said. "Miranda is missing. Her things are also gone. We have no idea where she could be. Did she say anything to any of you that might give us a clue as to where to look?"

By now the four girls were awake. "You mean, she ran away?" asked Samantha in horror. "We have a concert tomorrow. She's first chair in the flute section."

"I'm pretty sure my mom's more worried about Miranda's safety than she is the concert," pointed out Alicia.

"I'm sorry. You're right," said Samantha, chagrined. "I just can't believe that Miranda would run away. She seemed fine during rehearsal. She sits right next to me. And she was fine during bowling and dinner."

"Did she say anything to any of you that might give you a clue as to where she would go? Did she mention going to a store or getting a snack or anything?" asked Isabela.

All four girls shook their heads negatively. They had no idea where Miranda might be. The only thing that gave Isabela any hope was when Samantha mentioned that Miranda was excited to play in the concert the following day. Wherever Miranda had headed to, she planned on being back for the concert.

Isabela quickly checked the other three girls' rooms. She had even less success there. None of the girls had any idea where Miranda could have gone. The only other helpful thing she learned was from Kayla who told Isabela that Miranda was extremely unhappy in Richfield. Also, Miranda hated her hair dyed black, and she hated her eyebrow piercing, but she kept them both because it bugged her aunt.

Once she was finished checking the girls' rooms, Isabela went to the lobby. Mr. Jacobs and Javier were already there. Isabela sank down into the couch next to Javier.

"Did you guys learn anything?" she asked hopefully.

"Nothing." Mr. Jacobs shook his head somberly. "No one has any idea where she could be. What about you?"

Isabela quickly informed the two men of the little bit of information she had gleaned from the girls. She gnawed anxiously on the knuckle of her index finger.

"I just don't know what to do next," said Isabela. "I mean, we can go to bed and hope that Miranda shows up by morning, but what if she ran away? What if she got kidnapped? I realize I'm jumping to worst case scenarios, but I'm worried."

"I'm worried also," said Mr. Jacobs. "I think we need to contact her aunt and see if she's heard from her. Also, it might be time to contact the police."

"I wish we had a car," spoke up Javier. "We could drive around looking for her."

"That's actually a good idea," said Mr. Jacobs excitedly. "I have friends here in Rexburg from the music program. I'll call one of them to see if we can borrow their car."

"While you do that, I'll call Miranda's aunt. I work with Zoe, so I know her well enough to call her and tell her what's going on."

"And I guess I'll just sit here and worry," said Javier helplessly.

"How about if you go talk to the front desk clerk. See if he noticed Miranda leaving with anyone," suggested Mr. Jacobs.

The teacher pulled out his phone and scrolled through his pictures. A second later there was a chime on Javier's phone. "I just sent you a picture that has Miranda in it," he told Javier.

Javier nodded and headed to the front desk. Isabela pulled out her phone and called Zoe. The phone rang several times before Zoe finally answered. Her voice sounded tired. Isabela was positive that she had woken the woman.

"Zoe, this is Isabela San Pedro."

"I know who it is. If you're calling to see if I can work, the answer is no. I specifically requested this weekend off so I could get some things done around the house." Zoe spoke sharply into the phone.

"I'm not calling about work, Zoe," said Isabela softly. "I'm chaperoning the music trip. I'm calling about Miranda. She's missing."

"Missing? What do you mean missing?" Zoe's voice lost its sharpness, and Isabela could hear her concern for her niece.

"We took the kids bowling, and then brought them back to the hotel. No one has seen her since we returned. She told the girls she was rooming with that she was switching rooms, but the girls in the room she supposedly switched to were unaware she was saying that. Her stuff is missing. We have no idea where she could have gone." Isabela paused. She could hear Zoe breathing heavily on the other end of the phone.

"I don't know what to say. Should I drive up there? It would take me almost six hours to get there. Have you called the police? What should I do?" Isabela could tell that Zoe was fighting to hold back the tears as she spoke.

"No, we haven't called the police yet. We were hoping you might be able to give us an idea of where she could be. And no, I don't think it's necessary for you to drive up here. At least not yet," replied Isabela.

"I have no idea where she could be," said Zoe.

"Do you think she ran away, back to Phoenix?" asked Isabela.

"That wouldn't make sense," Zoe replied. "We're closer to Phoenix in Richfield. Besides, there's nothing for her in Phoenix. Her mom died in a car accident, so there's no family to live with."

"What about friends?" asked Isabela.

"She has friends in Phoenix, but none close enough to stay with. That's one of the reasons why she's living with me now. Her best friend graduated and left for college. A couple months later, the friend's family moved to Texas."

"Okay, so we know she didn't run back to Arizona," said Isabela thoughtfully. "What about the friend. Do you know where she is?"

"No, I don't," answered Zoe. "Oh, I'm so worried about her. Maybe I should come. I've been a bad aunt. I've been so caught up in my own pain, I didn't pay enough attention to Miranda. I can't lose her too. What should I do?"

"Try calling her and sending her texts," said Isabela. "For now, stay there in case she tries to contact you."

"Okay, I will. If I think of anything that might help, I'll let you know," Zoe promised.

Isabela hung up the phone and rejoined Mr. Jacobs and Javier. Both men looked glum.

"The desk clerk didn't see anything," said Javier.

"A friend of mine is coming in a few minutes to drive around Rexburg with us to see if we can find Miranda," added Mr. Jacobs.

"Do you think we should contact the police?" asked Isabela.

"I think we need to," said Mr. Jacobs with a sigh. "How did her aunt take it?"

"She's upset and worried, but not angry with us. She's more angry with herself for not being more aware of Miranda," replied Isabela. "She said that she'd contact us if she hears anything."

"You spent quite a bit of time talking to Miranda," said Javier. "Did she say anything at all that might give us a clue?"

"No, she didn't. We just talked about boring stuff. I can't think of anything that..." Isabela's voice suddenly trailed off.

"What is it?" asked Mr. Jacob's.

"Oh, my gosh! I think I know where she is!" Isabela exclaimed. "We might need the police to help locate her though."

"Where?" asked Mr. Jacobs and Javier in unison.

"I think she went to see her best friend. What's Miranda's last name?" asked Isabela.

"Murray," replied Mr. Jacobs. "How does that help us?"

"Miranda told me that she and her friend Caitlin have the same last name. If we find Caitlin, I'll bet we find Miranda!" said Isabela excitedly.

We don't even know what state Caitlin is in," pointed out Mr. Jacobs, "and I'm sure there are hundreds of Caitlin Murrays in the world."

"But how many Caitlin Murrays are attending Brigham Young University Idaho?" asked Isabela.

"I thought Miranda said she didn't know what college her friend was going to," said Javier.

"I think she lied to me," said Isabela. "When I asked her where Caitlin went to college she said 'ida…know.' I think she started to say Idaho but caught herself."

"Okay, so how do we find Caitlin Murray?" asked Javier.

"We could call the police," replied Isabela. "I hate to involve them, but they have the resources to find Caitlin if she's really here. Our only other option would be if we knew someone at the university who would be willing to check the university records for us and get us an address."

"I actually know someone," said Mr. Jacobs excitedly. "The guy who is coming with the car works for the music department at the university. I'll bet he knows someone who works in the office who would be willing to help us find Caitlin."

"And if not, we call the police," said Isabela.

At that moment, a man came rushing into the lobby. He had on a navy parka and jeans. It was obvious he had dressed hurriedly. He was wearing snow boots, but the left boot was black, the other dark brown.

"Les! Did you find her?" asked the man as he hurried across the lobby.

"Not yet," said Mr. Jacobs, "but we think we have an idea where she might be. We think she might be visiting a friend attending the university. Her name is Caitlin Murray. Do you know anyone that could help us get Caitlin's contact information?"

"My wife," said the man. "She works for the registrar's office. Let me call her."

"By the way," said Mr. Jacobs, "this is John Phillips, head of the music department. John, this is Isabela and Javier, my chaperones."

"It's nice to meet you," said John, eyeing Isabela and Javier. "That's pretty cool that you could get a married couple for your chaperones. It saves you the price of a room. I was never that lucky when I taught high school."

"Oh!" exclaimed Javier. "We aren't married. We aren't even dating!"

"Oops! Sorry about that," replied John. "I just assumed. Let me call my wife."

Isabela was glad that Javier had corrected John, that John knew the two of them weren't a couple, but for some reason, she'd felt a twinge of sadness when Javier stated that they weren't even dating. What was wrong with her? Why did she feel disappointed? She didn't even like Javier. Did she?

Chapter 13

John placed a call to his wife. Twenty minutes later she had a phone number for a student named Caitlin Murray. Because Mrs. Phillips was reluctant to give out the information, she agreed to call Caitlin herself. A few minutes later, Isabela's phone rang. The Caller ID showed that it was Miranda calling.

"Where are you?" asked Isabela as soon as she answered the phone.

"I'm at my friend's house. I'm just visiting with her." Isabela could hear the contrition in Miranda's voice. "I'm sorry everyone was so worried."

"Text me the address so that we can come to you," said Isabela. "It's better that we talk in person than over the phone."

"Okay, said Miranda. "I'm sorry."

Once the text arrived, the adults piled into Mr. Phillips's car. "Do you think it's safe to leave the kids alone at the hotel?" asked Isabela.

"They're all asleep," said Mr. Jacobs, "and they all have my phone number. They can call us if they need us. We won't be gone long."

Fifteen minutes later, the car pulled up in front of an apartment complex. The parking lot was filled with older vehicles. Most of them looked like they would be lucky to make it across town. Isabela grinned, remembering her own days of being a poor college student.

The address was on the second floor of the complex. When they reached the door, they saw that the lights were still on. At least, they wouldn't be waking the occupants. Mr. Jacobs knocked softly on the door so as not to disturb the neighbors.

A tall girl with brown hair and matching brown eyes opened the door. When she smiled, Isabela noticed that she had a bit of an overbite.

"Does Caitlin Murray live here?" asked Isabela.

"Yes, I'm Caitlin," said the girl. Her voice trembled slightly as she answered. It was obvious that she wasn't used to being in trouble.

"Is Miranda still here?" asked Mr. Jacobs as the group stepped inside. He closed the door behind them, shutting out the chill winter air.

"I'm here." Miranda stepped out of the kitchen. Her hair was several shades lighter, and the eyebrow piercing was gone.

"One of my roommates went to beauty school before she decided to come to BYU-I," explained Caitlin when she noticed the surprised expression on the adults' faces. "We decided to lighten Miranda's hair."

"I don't know whether to yell at you or hug you," said Mr. Jacobs to Miranda. "You have no idea how worried we've been about you."

"I'm sorry," she said. She stared at her feet as she spoke. "I just really wanted to spend some time with Caitlin. We couldn't hang out during the day because I had rehearsal, and she had work and classes."

"Why didn't you just ask if you could hang out with her?" asked Isabela.

"I didn't think anyone would notice I was missing," explained Miranda. "I planned to be back in time for breakfast at the hotel."

"That still doesn't explain why you didn't just ask," pointed out Javier.

"I was afraid you'd say no," Miranda admitted.

"I'd have said yes," said Mr. Jacobs. "I've let kids go stay other places before. You just have to let me know."

"Did anyone contact Miranda's aunt?" asked Javier.

"I called her," said Miranda. "She knows that I'm safe and that you guys were coming to get me."

"I'd better let her know we have you, just the same," spoke up Isabela.

She pulled her phone out of the pocket of her coat and wrote a quick text. *We have Miranda. She is safe.* Isabela hit send.

A moment later her phone chimed. *Thanks for letting me know!*

"Do I have to go back with you guys?" asked Miranda. "I know I do because I'm in trouble, but I haven't seen Caitlin since before my mom died. I really want to spend the night here. I'm close enough to the university that I can walk there."

Mr. Jacobs shook his head, "I'm not sure what to do. All the kids are asleep at the hotel. I hate to disturb them by having you go into one of the rooms. On the other hand, school policy says I can't let you stay here without written permission from your guardian. Besides that, you're in so much trouble."

Isabela spoke up, "I have an idea. Could you two girls step into the kitchen for a moment, so the rest of us can discuss this privately?"

Caitlin and Miranda nodded their heads in agreement. As soon as they were out of the front room, Isabela turned to the three men. "I really feel for Miranda. I think that emotionally, it's good for her to spend some time with Caitlin. Plus, if we take her back it will wake the girls in her room when she goes in. On the other hand, she definitely needs some consequences."

"So, what do you suggest we do?" asked Mr. Jacobs.

"Let's let her spend the night here if it's okay with her aunt. Then when we get back to Richfield, we'll decide what sort of consequences she has to face. Maybe in-house suspension or cafeteria duty? Or a report? I don't know, but we have a six-hour bus ride back to Richfield to discuss it with her and come up with a fitting consequence."

"I like it," said Mr. Jacobs slowly. "And we aren't really rewarding her for running off. I would have let her stay with Caitlin if she had just asked."

The girls were called back into the front room. Mr. Jacobs explained what had been decided. Miranda made a quick phone call to her aunt and was given permission to spend the night with Caitlin. Everything was settled with Miranda promising to be on time for rehearsal.

After Mr. Phillips dropped them off at the hotel, Mr. Jacobs said goodnight and headed to his room. Javier stood in the lobby and gazed at Isabela.

"I don't know about you," he said, "but I'm too wound up to sleep. Would you care to join me for some hot cocoa?" He gestured toward the hot chocolate machine in the corner of the lobby.

"Sure, that sounds relaxing," said Isabela.

After they had their cups of cocoa, the pair sat down on the couch in front of the gas fireplace. Isabela noticed that Javier was sitting a tad closer to her than necessary, or maybe it was she who was sitting closer. Either way, she was surprised to discover that she liked the closeness.

"That was pretty smart the way you figured out where Miranda," was commented Javier.

Isabela blushed at the compliment. "I was just putting two and two together," she replied modestly.

"I don't think I'd have figured it out," Javier admitted.

"You would have," she assured him.

The two fell into a comfortable silence. They quietly sipped their hot cocoa and watched the flames in the fireplace dance against the logs.

"I'm glad you came on this trip," said Javier abruptly. "It's been fun."

"Yes, it has," agreed Isabela. "Well, minus the part where we lost a kid. They may never ask us to chaperone again."

"Well, to be fair, we only lost one kid out of 34," said Javier. "We kept track of the other 33 kids. That means we still had 97 percent of the kids we started out with. We're still in the A range for chaperones."

Isabela burst out laughing at his reasoning. "Next time we lose a kid, we'll just point that out to Mr. Jacobs. In fact, as long as we're in the C range, we're still passing as chaperones."

"If we return with 75 percent of the kids, that makes us average chaperones because C is average. I had no idea that the average chaperone lost 25 percent of the kids they started out with," chuckled Javier.

"They say you learn something new every day," said Isabela. She tried unsuccessfully to hold back a large yawn.

"Am I that boring?" teased Javier.

"No, I'm just starting to feel tired," she admitted.

"I was joking. I'm getting a little sleepy too. I should probably get to bed soon. I have a lot of work I need to do tomorrow," he replied.

"What exactly are you doing on your computer?" she asked him curiously.

"It's top secret," he said. "I can't tell you that."

"You are so frustrating," she said. "Why do you keep giving me that lame excuse? Are you embarrassed about what you're working on or something?"

"Why do you keep asking if you don't like my answer?" he countered.

"I guess I'm just curious," she replied.

"You know what they say about curiosity and the cat," he said.

"You know what, I'm just going to head to bed. Forget I said anything. I was just interested, but now I realize that I'm really not." Before Javier could reply, Isabela marched out of the lobby.

Once inside her room, Isabela leaned against the door. She fought back the tears that suddenly formed in her eyes. Why did she feel so hurt and so lost inside? Why did this man bring out so many emotions in her? She wanted to hate him like she used to, but a tiny part of her would not let that happen any longer.

Chapter 14

The next morning at breakfast, Isabela was eating a bagel and cream cheese when Javier walked up. He set a glass of juice next to her. "I thought you might be thirsty," he said. "I'm sorry about last night.

Before Isabela could reply, he walked away. He sat down at a table with Alejandro, Alicia, and several other teenagers. The group was laughing about something. Chagrined, Isabela looked down at her bagel. Had she overreacted last night? She couldn't be sure. The only thing she was sure of was that she didn't like fighting with Javier, but she wasn't sure how to mend things between them.

Later as the group loaded up onto the bus, Isabela made up her mind to talk to Javier and apologize for overreacting again and for being nosy.

However, when she got on the bus, he and Mr. Jacobs were talking animatedly about something. Isabela felt too embarrassed to join them, and she certainly didn't want to apologize in front of the band teacher. It would have to wait until later.

Once they arrived at the university, the students hurried into the practice hall. In addition to their instruments, they were also carrying their concert clothing. That evening there would be a concert, allowing the students to show off what they had learned. Families were invited to attend. Students who lived within a two-hour radius generally had parents who showed up for the concert. Those who lived farther away didn't have much representation. Since Richfield was almost six hours away, Mr. Jacobs didn't expect any parents to show up for the concert.

Isabela followed the students into the practice hall. She found a chair off in the corner and pulled out the book she had been reading. She was almost finished with it. Luckily, she had brought its sequel, so she wouldn't be bored that afternoon.

Javier pulled out his laptop and set up his workspace on a nearby table. Whatever it was that he was doing, he seemed pretty serious about it.

Isabela couldn't help but be curious, but she wouldn't ask again. She was tired of being rebuffed. Besides, it really wasn't any of her business. Mostly, though, she didn't want to have bad feelings between them. If he didn't want to talk about his work, she wouldn't bring it up again.

Isabela glanced around the room. Students were still getting instruments out and warmed up. She should apologize to Javier now. This would be the perfect time to tell him she was sorry for how she had been acting. She stood up from her chair just as the coordinator stood in front of the band and called them to attention. Isabela sat back down.

"Today, I have an announcement that concerns you kids and the chaperones, so if I could get everyone to listen, I'd appreciate it."

The room quieted down immediately as everyone turned their attention to the coordinator. Even the heating system was silent.

"This morning, we have a small snack area just down the hall from us. We have juice, hot cocoa, and some doughnuts. When we take our morning break, you students can go down there and help yourselves to some snacks. That's our way of telling you thank you for being so cooperative and so professional. Chaperones, you are welcome to visit our little snack area anytime and bring the snacks back with you to eat while our students practice."

The room filled with appreciative murmurs for a few seconds before becoming quiet again. The coordinator explained the practice schedule and how things would work for the concert that night. Finally, she finished and turned the time over to the band director.

Isabela sighed and leaned back in her chair. It would be at least two hours before the first break. She would have to wait until then to apologize to Javier. Even then, she might not get the opportunity, depending on how many students were around.

Isabela tried to concentrate on her book, but it was difficult. She was acutely aware of Javier's presence on the other side of the room. She could see him working busily on his computer. She wondered if he was having as hard of a time concentrating as she was. He didn't seem to be though. Even from this distance, she could see his fingers flying quickly along his keyboard.

The instruments fell silent for a moment. The band director clapped his hands to show the students the rhythm he expected for the piece they were working on. Once he finished clapping, he had the students clap along with him. Isabela could see that many of them had their toes tapping as well. Once the clapping stopped the director instructed the students to play that section of the piece again.

During the momentary lull while the students picked up their instruments, Isabela's cell phone chimed. She'd forgotten to turn it off. The sound seemed to echo throughout the silence of the practice hall. The band director turned and glared at the chaperones. He scanned the room, as though looking for the guilty culprit.

Isabela tried to keep her face impassive, but she felt her cheeks blush slightly. Around her, she felt that other chaperones were staring at her judgmentally. She tried not to look guilty.

"Chaperones," said the band director loudly, "remember to turn off your phones so as not to distract our fine musicians up here." He gave the group one more glare before turning back to the students.

Once everything had settled down and the band was playing a lively march, Isabela reached casually for her phone. She surreptitiously checked her phone. The text was from Javier.

I really am sorry. Meet me in the snack area. Please? So we can talk.

Isabela glanced up at Javier. He was watching her expectantly. She smiled and nodded as she slipped her phone into her pocket and exited the practice hall. As she stood, she saw Javier close his laptop and place it in its carry bag.

A few minutes later, the two of them were seated next to each other at a small table. They each had a glazed doughnut and cup of hot chocolate.

"Sorry for the text," said Javier as he took a sip of his cocoa. "I didn't mean to get you in trouble."

"That's my fault for forgetting to turn the sound off," Isabela replied with a laugh. "Lesson learned. I'll bet I never forget again."

"It made me doublecheck my phone, that's for sure," said Javier.

The two fell silent for a moment, unsure what else to say. Finally, Isabela took a deep breath and spoke, "I'm sorry for overreacting. Again. And for being nosy. It's not any of my business what you're doing on the computer."

"I shouldn't be so closemouthed about it," said Javier. "It's really not that big of a deal, I guess."

"Now you make me want to ask again, and I just promised you I'd stop being nosy. You have to help me out here. You can't tempt me like that," laughed Isabela.

"I guess that would pique your curiosity a little," said Javier with a wry chuckle.

"Just a little." Isabela paused then added, "I really am sorry though. Please forgive me?"

"There's nothing to forgive," said Javier. "It's my own insecurities. I always tell people I'm working on something top secret when they ask. I'm kind of embarrassed to tell them the truth."

"You're making me curious again," said Isabela. "I'll keep my promise to stop being nosy, but you have to stop torturing me."

"Isa," said Javier, "I don't mind telling you what I'm working on. I'm just not used to telling people."

"Are you embarrassed?" asked Isabela. "Are you running an online dating site for cat ladies and the men who secretly want to be cat men?"

Javier started laughing, "No, but I'll bet a dating site like that could make money."

Isabela laughed too, "They say there's someone out there for everyone."

"The truth is," Javier paused for a moment, "I'm writing a book. It's what I do for a living. I write. But I don't like lots of attention, so I usually tell people that what I'm doing is top secret. I have a lot of people convinced I must work for the government."

"You're writing a book? That's awesome. Have you had any books published?" asked Isabela.

"A few. I just don't like being in the spotlight. I write under a pen name," he replied.

"Really? Do you mind if I ask what books you've written? Maybe I've read one of them," said Isabela.

"Oh, you have," laughed Javier.

"How can you be so sure?" asked Isabela. "Unless the book you wrote was a nursing textbook. If that's the case, ugh. Boring!"

"The book you're reading right now is one I wrote," said Javier slowly.

"YOU wrote the book I'm reading? I love that book! You should be proud of yourself, not trying to hide who you are!" exclaimed Isabela.

"I'm not embarrassed about the books I write," explained Javier.

"Then what is it?" asked Isabela curiously, raising her eyebrows slightly as she spoke.

"I just don't like all of the attention. It makes me feel embarrassed and uncomfortable. That's why I use a pen name. Most people don't recognize me from my picture, and I enjoy the anonymity," he explained.

Isabela grinned, "No wonder the picture of the author on my book looked so familiar! It was you, only in the photo, you don't have a mustache or beard."

"This is my disguise," replied Javier. "Do you like it?"

"Actually, yes I do," said Isabela softly.

Before she could stop herself, she reached over and gently caressed Javier's face. He reached up and took her hand. For just a moment, it was as though they were frozen in time. Suddenly, they both seemed to be aware of their surroundings. Javier let go of Isabela's hand, which she quickly dropped to her lap.

"Umm…well, for what it's worth, I really like the book," Isabela stammered.

"Thanks," Javier said with a wry grin. "Do you mind if I ask you a personal question?"

"I guess it depends on what it is," said Isabela with a shrug. "I mean, if you're going to ask me if I've ever created a more awkward situation than just now, the answer is no."

Javier chuckled at her response. "Well, I hadn't thought of that question, but I'm glad you told me. Actually, I was wondering how long you've been single."

Isabela took a deep breath. She didn't mind talking about her first marriage, at least not much. "We separated when Alicia was two. He wasn't a nice person. I was better off without him. He isn't involved in Alicia's life at all, and that suits me just fine. What about you?"

"Alejandro's mom left me when he was four. She said she didn't want to be tied down with a little kid. She left me for a guy who promised her more excitement. I haven't heard from her since." He fell silent for a moment. "It was hard on Alejandro. She didn't spend much time with him as it was, but she was still his mom, and he missed her when she left. After that, I vowed I would never get into another relationship again."

Isabela was surprised at the sudden pang of disappointment she felt when she heard him state that he would never be involved with another woman. She hadn't even considered a relationship with him. Yet, for some reason, she felt sad when she realized that she didn't have a chance of building a future with him.

"I don't think Alicia even noticed that her dad was gone, or if she did, she was probably happy. When he was around, he didn't pay much attention to her except to yell at her," Isabela spoke matter-of-factly. Deep down, she knew she was interested in Javier, but she didn't want him to know that.

"I don't understand people sometimes," said Javier. "I could never be mean to my wife or child, and I could never just leave my son or daughter."

"I know what you mean," agreed Isabela.

"How do you think the band is sounding?" asked Javier, changing the subject.

"Really good," said Isabela. "When they first started rehearsing, I wasn't sure they would be able to learn all the music, but they've progressed remarkably well."

Javier nodded his agreement. "The band director is a good one. He expects perfection from these kids, and I think he's going to get it."

"I do too," said Isabela. "Of course, Mr. Jacobs has taught our Richfield kids well. I think they already knew the march they're doing before we got here."

"I know that Alejandro knew it. He practiced it a bunch at home," said Javier.

"So did Alicia. It's a fun piece to listen to. I can't remember who the composer is," Isabela replied. "I know he's someone famous."

Javier grinned, "The composer is John Phillips Sousa."

"Wait!" said Isabela. "Mr. Jacob's friend's name is…"

"John Phillips," laughed Javier, "and he became a band director. I wonder if his parents knew of John Phillips Sousa when they named him."

As the two talked, Isabela felt a glow of happiness spreading within her chest. Javier was so easygoing and so much fun to talk to that she felt completely at ease. She found herself wondering why Javier was still single, in spite of his vow never to be involved in a relationship again. He was handsome and had a fun personality. Surely women flocked to him, but maybe he spent all his free time focused on raising his son. Or maybe, she mused, he was like her, and preferred being single to having his heart broken again.

A burst of voices interrupted their conversation which had morphed to a lively discussion about favorite vacation spots. Isabela glanced up to see a crowd of students heading towards them. She glanced at her watch. She and Javier had been visiting for almost two hours.

"I can't believe we've been out here all this time," she exclaimed.

"Me either," he admitted. "Time flies when you're having fun, I guess."

Alicia and Alejandro walked up to the table where the two were seated. "Have you been out here this whole time?" asked Alicia.

"No?" said Isabela hesitantly. "Maybe? Possibly?"

"Did anyone miss us?" asked Javier.

"Yes, they did," said Alejandro. "One of the kids got sick. They were looking for a chaperone to go get him some ibuprofen and let him lie down in one of the empty rooms."

"Oh, no!" exclaimed Isabela. "Are you serious? Which kid?"

"I'm joking," laughed Alejandro. "No one got sick. I doubt anyone missed you except for me and Alicia and that's just because you're our parents. We always try to keep track of you."

"You do?" asked Javier.

"Yes, of course," said Alicia. "We don't want to lose you."

"That's so sweet." Isabela smiled lovingly at her daughter.

"After all, you have all the money that we need for meals and snacks and things," explained Alicia.

"Wow! Now the truth comes out!" exclaimed Isabela, pretending to be offended.

Alicia and Alejandro laughed and got in line at the doughnut table. "I suppose we should go back inside for the rest of morning practice," said Isabela.

"Yeah, I think so," agreed Javier. "But I enjoyed just sitting out here talking. It was fun getting to know you better, Isa." Isabela felt a glow of warmth at the use of the nickname, which she had begun to associate as his pet name for her.

The two made their way back into the practice hall. Without saying anything, Javier moved his stuff so that he was sitting closer to Isabela. She smiled as he plugged in his laptop. She couldn't believe that she actually knew a famous author.

The rest of morning practice went by quickly and before she knew it, the band director was dismissing the students to go get lunch. The coordinator stood up and reminded the students that even though they had an hour, it wasn't really a full hour. They needed to be in their seats, ready to play by 12:55.

As the group made their way outside, Isabela realized she'd forgotten her wallet in her backpack. "Go ahead," she told the others. "I'll catch up."

Isabela hurried and grabbed her wallet out of a hidden pouch in her backpack. She wasn't worried about it getting stolen, but she needed it so she could buy lunch for her and Alicia.

When she stepped back into the lobby, she saw that everyone was gone. She felt a stab of disappointment that no one had waited, even though she'd told them to go ahead. She'd hoped that Alicia at least would wait.

Even as she was thinking these thoughts, Isabela realized that she wasn't really disappointed that her daughter didn't wait for her. She had hoped that Javier would be waiting for her, but of course, he would feel obligated to stay with the group as a chaperone.

As Isabela stepped up to the doors, a flash of movement in the corner of her eye caught her attention. Javier was standing next to the Ficus tree in the lobby of the building.

"I waited for you," he explained when she raised her eyebrows questioningly. "The kids are all with Mr. Jacobs. I figured he could handle them for a few minutes. After all, we had them all morning."

"Yes, all morning, except for the part where we played hooky," laughed Isabela. "You didn't need to wait though."

"I wanted to," said Javier.

Isabela smiled and stepped outside the building. It had started snowing again. Giant flakes swirled around her. The sidewalk was already covered in snow, almost completely obliterating the tracks of the students who had left just a few minutes before.

As they started across the campus, Isabela's foot hit a slick spot under the snow. She lost her balance. Javier quickly grabbed her arm to keep her from falling. Once she was steady though, instead of letting go, he took her hand and led her across the snowy sidewalks.

He's just holding my hand because he doesn't want me to fall. He's just being a gentleman, Isabela kept repeating to herself. *He isn't doing this because he has feelings for me. He's just a nice guy. That's all.*

Logically, Isabela knew there was nothing between her and Javier, but if she was honest with herself, she wished that there was something. She was starting to fall for him. He was kind and fun and incredibly handsome. But from their earlier talk, she also knew that he had no intention of being in a relationship.

Still, she couldn't deny the warmth that she felt inside as she held his hand. It was almost as though an electrical current went from his hand into hers. She had never felt anything like this before.

All too soon, they reached the building where the cafeteria was located. Javier dropped her hand to open the door for her. She stepped inside. She felt like an awkward teenager as she walked next to him down the hallway. She let her hand dangle at her side in case he wanted to hold her hand again. Much to her disappointment, Javier didn't take her hand.

"Thank you for helping me get safely across the walks," she told him as they entered the cafeteria.

Javier looked at her strangely. "You're welcome," he replied stiffly.

The air suddenly felt chilly, but Isabela was unsure what she had done to change things between them. Had holding her hand meant something to him after all? Did it make him think that she hadn't felt anything when she thanked him for the help across the walks? Why did he have to be so darn complicated?

They joined Mr. Jacobs for lunch. "It's going to be a late night tonight," he informed them as they sat down. "And the bus is going to be extra crowded."

"Why is that?" asked Javier. "We had plenty of room on the way up, and a couple of the kids said they might have parents coming."

"It's snowing so hard, that I doubt we have any parents trying to make the trip," said Mr. Jacobs. "Six hours is a long drive even when it's good weather."

"You have a good point there," agreed Javier.

"But that's not the problem. I just talked to Tim Dahl. He had lunch with us the first day," said Mr. Jacobs.

"Oh, I remember him," spoke up Isabela. "He's the band teacher at South Sevier High School."

"That's right," said Mr. Jacobs.

"What about him?" asked Javier. "Is there a problem?"

"Yeah, their bus broke down," said Mr. Jacobs. "The district could send up another bus for them, but like I said, it's a six-hour drive. They're wondering if we would have room on our bus for the South Sevier kids."

"How many kids do they have?" asked Javier.

"Only eighteen plus Mr. Dahl and another chaperone. I told them they could ride with us. It will be crowded but better than them waiting for another bus to come. The bus they came in is waiting on parts, so it won't be fixed until next week," replied Mr. Jacobs.

"We'll manage," said Isabela. "It won't kill the juniors and seniors to have to double up on seats."

"I'm afraid we'll all have to double up," said Mr. Jacobs. "But it's our best option."

Isabela felt a sudden thrill rush through her at the prospect of sharing a seat with Javier, but then just as quickly, she felt deflated. Javier and Alejandro would probably share a seat, and she would share with Alicia. That made more sense than having the two chaperones share with each other.

She stole a quick glance at Javier and caught him watching her. He gave her a quick smile and a wink. She blushed furiously and turned her attention to her salad, letting her hair fall down next to her cheek. She hoped Javier didn't notice the reddening of her cheeks.

When lunch ended, they headed back outside into the snowstorm. "Take my arm so you don't fall," suggested Javier and they stepped onto the sidewalk.

Isabela hesitated a second before taking his arm. Even though he had offered, she didn't want to appear too forward. She knew that he was just being a gentleman and offering his arm so she would be safe, but she was taking it because she wanted to feel the closeness of his touch. Still, Javier didn't know that's how she felt. In his mind, she was just taking it so that she could safely get from the cafeteria back to the music building.

Isabela kept a firm grip on Javier's arm. She liked the feeling of security she got from it, and that secure feeling wasn't just because he kept her from slipping. She realized that something about his close proximity made her feel safe. She reveled in the feeling for just a moment before she reminded herself that he was just being a gentleman. He had no feelings for her.

All too soon, they were back at the music building, and she had to let go of his arm. She hated to do so, but short of faking an injury, she couldn't think of any reason to keep holding it.

She wished that he would say, "You can keep holding my arm if you want to," but of course, he remained silent.

For just a moment though, she allowed herself to enjoy the warmth she felt when she was with him. For just a split second, she fantasized what it would be like to be married to this man as Mr. Phillips had suggested. But just for a second, because she knew that he would never break his vow and become involved with someone, and she couldn't stand the thought of having her heart broken again.

Chapter 15

Afternoon practice took place in the concert hall. Chaperones were kindly asked to leave so that the concert would be a new experience for them.

"Please wait in our snack area," the coordinator told them. "If we need one of you, that's where we will come to find you."

Javier found a table to set his laptop on. "I have a deadline coming up," he told her apologetically. "I promised my agent I'd have this novel finished by the end of the month; otherwise, I'd just sit and talk to you."

"That's okay," said Isabela. "I want to finish reading this book. I'm at an exciting part. The girl just got kidnapped and…" Her voice trailed off, and she started laughing. "Well, I guess it's enough to say that it's an exciting book."

"Thank you," said Javier with a smile.

Isabela found that just being in Javier's presence was enough. Each time she turned a page in the book he had written, she allowed her eyes to glide over and look at him. A few times, she caught him looking back at her. Whenever that happened, he would smile and wink, and she would try unsuccessfully not to blush.

Dinner that evening was set up in the practice hall where the kids had rehearsed for the past two days. The music department had hired the university's culinary department to cater a meal for the students and their chaperones. The meal consisted of deli sandwiches, potato salad, macaroni salad, and brownies for dessert.

As students finished their dinners, they were instructed to change into their concert clothing and go into the concert hall. Concert attire consisted of a white shirt and black pants or black skirt. Boys were required to wear a black tie. As the students from the various schools came back into the room wearing their concert clothing, Isabela found they had transformed from gangly teenagers to serious musicians.

Javier and Isabela made their way into the concert hall. They chose seats near the front in the center row. A few moments later, Mr. Jacobs joined them, sitting next to Isabela. Around them the concert hall began to fill up.

"Do you mind if I join you?" asked a familiar voice on the other side of Mr. Jacobs.

Startled, Isabela turned to see who the speaker was. To her surprise, it was Zoe, Miranda's aunt.

"Yes, please do!" exclaimed Mr. Jacobs, patting the seat next to him.

"I can't believe you came all this way," said Isabela. "The storm's horrible out there."

"It wasn't really that stormy until I got to the Utah-Idaho border," said Zoe. "Of course, if I'd known how bad the roads would be after I crossed into Idaho, I might have just stayed home."

"Did you just get into Rexburg?" asked Isabela.

"No, I left early this morning. I've been here a few hours. I got a hotel here in Rexburg. After the fright we had with Miranda last night, I realized that I've been ignoring her. I've been too caught up in my own grief, missing my sister. She and I were best friends, but I need to channel that friendship and love into raising Miranda. So, I came for her concert. The flute and music are important to her. She doesn't know I'm here. It's a surprise."

Zoe smiled as she spoke. It was the first time that Isabela had seen her smile in months. She suddenly realized how much pain Zoe must have been going through.

"I'm glad you came. Miranda will be so excited that you're here. She told me that you two used to be close," said Isabela.

"We were, and I want to regain that closeness," said Zoe.

"I'm assuming that Miranda won't be riding the bus home then," said Mr. Jacobs. He reached into his backpack and pulled out a release form for Zoe to sign, stating that she would be taking Miranda after the concert.

"We'll spend tonight here in Rexburg. Then I want to spend the rest of the weekend in Salt Lake. We'll do some good, old-fashioned shopping. I might even let her skip school on Monday. Tuesday, she can deal with the consequences of scaring all of us half to death," explained Zoe.

The lights of the concert hall dimmed, signaling that the concert was about to start. Isabela glanced around. Almost all of the seats were filled. Even though it was a stormy night in Rexburg, many families had traveled to see the young musicians play.

The program coordinator stood up and welcomed everyone to the concert. "Now, we have a couple of solo numbers and a duet in our concert tonight. These kids who will be doing these special numbers learned their pieces while still at home. They came here and auditioned for the opportunity to perform tonight. I think you'll be very pleased to hear these numbers, and I think you'll agree that we have the best of the best performing with us tonight."

"That's nice," whispered Isabela to Mr. Jacobs. "I didn't realize they did soloists also."

"They usually don't," he whispered back. "This is a new thing they're trying, but I think it's something they'll do again next year."

The program coordinator was introducing the band director. Once his list of accomplishments was outlined, she turned the stage over to him. He was met with wild applause, particularly from the members of the band. It was obvious that the students loved him.

Isabela sat back as the first number began. It was a cheerful piece that reminded her of warm weather and hiking in the mountains. Next to her, she noticed Javier silently tapping his finger in rhythm to the music.

The piece ended and everyone applauded. As the applause died down, the band director turned and spoke into the mike. "This next number is our duet. We have two students here who play the oboe and clarinet. When they auditioned with this piece, we were all absolutely delighted, not just with how well they performed the music, but with how much character and personality they put into the performance. Coming from Richfield High School, in Richfield Utah, I give you Alicia San Pedro and Alejandro Varilla."

To the sound of the polite applause from the audience, Alejandro and Alicia stood from their chairs in the front row of the band and moved to the center of the stage. Neither one of them had their instruments. They stepped up to the microphone.

"We're going to be playing "Humoresque," said Alicia.

"This piece was composed by Doug Harville," added Alejandro.

"Where's your instrument?" Alicia asked Alejandro in a dramatic stage whisper.

"Where's yours?" he fired back.

"Oops!" she said laughing, then speaking back into the microphone she addressed the audience. "We're so nervous, we forgot to grab out instruments."

The audience chuckled appreciatively, but Isabela was frozen. It wasn't like Alicia to get nervous before a performance, but of course, she'd never played in front of such a large crowd before. And she'd never done a solo or a duet before. Isabela assumed the same held true for Alejandro. She glanced over at Javier. He appeared to be as nervous for the kids as she was.

"I didn't know they were going to do this," he whispered.

"Neither did I," she replied.

Mr. Jacobs leaned over and said softly, "They wanted to surprise both of you. I hope this doesn't backfire. I've never known them to be so nervous they would forget their instruments."

"Dr. Lawrence," said Alicia, addressing the band director, "would you mind handing me my oboe?"

"And could you get my clarinet while you're at it?" asked Alejandro.

Isabela tried unsuccessfully to breathe. This was just getting worse. Somehow it seemed wrong for the kids to be giving directions to a highly esteemed music professional.

"They'll be fine," whispered Javier.

"I hope so." Isabela clenched her hands together nervously.

Dr. Lawrence stepped over to the front row of musicians and took the instruments that were passed over to him. He walked back to Alicia and Javier who had been busily arranging their music on a stand. Dr. Lawrence handed them their instruments before stepping off to the side of the stage.

"I'm so nervous for them," murmured Isabela.

"Me too," whispered Javier. He reached over and took Isabela's hand. She held it tightly, grateful for the moral support.

Alejandro and Isabela looked at each other and began to play. The instruments squeaked loudly, causing the audience to wince. It seemed as though a tune might be coming out of them, but it was difficult to tell. Both kids looked down at their instruments in surprise. The audience squirmed uncomfortably. Isabela gripped Javier's hand a little tighter.

"What's wrong?" asked Alicia. "We've never sounded this bad before."

Alejandro looked down at his instrument and began laughing, "We have the wrong instruments. Dr. Lawrence got our instruments mixed up."

"He always did have a problem with woodwinds," remarked Alicia.

Several members of the audience began to chuckle as the two kids traded instruments. Dr. Lawrence was an accomplished oboist, something which had been brought out in his introduction. Those who had been paying attention appreciated the joke.

Alicia and Alejandro looked at each other and nodded and smiled. When they began playing, the result was fantastic. The piece they had chosen was aptly named "Humoresque" because it was a humorous piece, and the two kids performed it in such a way that kept the audience laughing.

They didn't hit any wrong notes. They played the music flawlessly, but they seemed to be speaking with each other through the notes: first competing, then insulting, then competing again.

When the number ended, the audience erupted into applause along with a few whoops. Several members of the audience stood as they clapped to show their appreciation. Isabela and Javier clapped loudly and joined those in the audience who were standing. Finally, the applause died down. Isabela and Javier sat back down. Alicia and Alejandro took one last bow and returned to their seats with the band.

When the applause began, Javier had dropped Isabela's hand so that they could clap. Now that the clapping was over, Isabela realized that her hand felt strangely empty. She missed the warmth of Javier's hand. She glanced over at him. He was staring at her. She smiled, and he returned her grin. He reached over and gently took her hand. This time it wasn't to lend moral support. It wasn't prompted by a bad case of nerves. This time, the message seemed to say, "I like you. Do you like me?" In response, Isabela squeezed his hand gently. Javier slowly caressed the side of her hand with his thumb. The movement sent a warm sensation throughout Isabela's entire body. She felt as though a block of ice that had once lived inside her was starting to melt. She looked over at Javier and smiled once more, just to let him know how contented she suddenly felt.

They held hands throughout the rest of the concert, only letting go when they needed to applaud. As soon as they were finished clapping, their hands found each other again. Isabela couldn't remember the last time she had felt so happy.

All too soon the concert ended and the two of them were caught up in the hustle and bustle of making sure all of the students had the chance to change into their travel clothing and that their concert attire and instruments were gathered and loaded on the bus. In addition to this, seating had to be rearranged to make room for the students and chaperones from South Sevier High School.

Finally, the bus was loaded, and everyone was seated. To her delight, Isabela ended up sharing a seat with Javier. When she'd boarded the bus, he had been sitting alone. His face lit up when he saw her, and he scooted over next to the window.

"You can sit here," he told her. He tried to sound casual, but there was no mistaking the hope in his voice.

"Thanks for saving me a place," she said to him as she sat down next to him. "I was afraid I'd have to climb into one of the overhead racks or ride with the luggage underneath."

"It would have to be underneath," Javier laughed. "The overhead racks are all full."

The bus shifted into gear and pulled out of the parking lot. The air was filled with the laughter of the students' voices. All around them, they could hear various students complimenting Alejandro and Alicia on their duet.

"They really did do a good job on the duet, didn't they?" said Isabela.

"Yes, but I'll admit I was a little nervous when they started to play and it sounded so horrible," laughed Javier.

"I was a nervous wreck," replied Isabela.

Javier reached over and took her hand. It was what she'd been hoping for. She'd kept her hand resting on her lap so that he could easily take it if he wanted to. Part of her had wanted to just take his hand, but that seemed too forward, and she was afraid of rejection. As he took her hand in hers, she sighed contentedly and leaned softly against him. He shifted his position slightly allowing her to cuddle up just a little closer to him.

They visited for a little while, but after a bit fell silent as the rest of the bus quieted down, and the students began falling asleep. In the darkness, Isabela felt Javier softly caress her arm with his free hand. Then she felt him gently kiss her on top of her head. Or maybe that was just her imagination as she too drifted off to sleep.

About an hour later, the bus pulled off at a gas station to allow students the chance to stretch their legs and use the restroom. Isabela woke as the bus pulled into the parking lot. She was suddenly acutely aware that she had fallen asleep against Javier's shoulder. Part of her wanted to stay there, but the other part of her suddenly felt embarrassed.

She sat up abruptly. "I'm sorry. I didn't mean to use you as a pillow," she laughed.

"That's okay," he replied with a chuckle. "At least you didn't drool too much."

"Did I drool?" she asked horrified.

"I'm only kidding," Javier replied. "If you did, I'm not aware of it."

"Well, you made a good pillow," she laughed.

"Great," said Javier. "If I ever decide to get a real job, I'll be sure to put that on my resume."

"You do that," agreed Isabela. "That might be the tipping point to set you above the other candidates."

"Do I have any other qualifications I should list?" asked Javier quietly, as he gently caressed the side of her hand.

Around them, students were exiting the bus, although several chose to remain in their seats and try to sleep.

"Well, I guess you could add that you are a good hand holder," said Isabela softly.

"Is that a good qualification to have?" asked Javier.

"I think it is," she told him.

"Hey, Dad!" called Alejandro from the front of the bus. "Can I have some money? I want to buy a snack."

The spell was broken. Javier found his coat and stood up. "I may as well get off and stretch my legs," he said. "Are you coming?"

Isabela stood as well. "Sure," she agreed. "Why not?"

When they got off the bus, they saw that it was snowing again. "Where are we?" asked Isabela, looking around.

"Salt Lake City," said Mr. Jacobs as he climbed down the steps of the bus. "So, we're halfway home."

"Yay," said Isabela. "At this rate we'll be home before 3:00 AM."

"Well, that's always a plus," laughed Mr. Jacobs.

"Let's go inside," suggested Javier. He gestured toward the convenience store. Alejandro was standing near the door gesturing for his father to hurry.

"I guess you're being summoned," laughed Isabela, pointing at Alejandro.

"I think you are too," said Javier. Just then Alicia stepped out of the store. When she saw her mother, she waved and went back inside.

Javier reached out and took Isabela's hand and together they walked across the parking lot to the little store. Isabela wondered if Mr. Jacobs had noticed them holding hands and what he thought about it if he had.

Once they were inside, Javier dropped Isabela's hand. She felt a rush of disappointment, and part of her couldn't help but wonder if he was embarrassed to have Alejandro see them holding hands. It would make perfect sense that maybe he didn't want Alejandro to know that he might be interested in someone.

Alicia wanted snacks also, and Isabela decided to buy herself a bottle of water. The two ended up in line ahead of Alejandro and Javier. Their purchases were surprisingly similar. While they waited, the four of them made small talk, mostly discussing how well Alejandro and Alicia had done with their duet.

"We had people asking how much time we spent practicing," Alicia laughed. "We told them that we spent hours because our parents forced us to practice."

"Yeah, we had people convinced that we're twins. It was awesome," put in Alejandro.

"Because we're the same age, and both of our names start with an A," explained Alicia.

"Then when you two started holding hands, we even had some of the Richfield kids thinking that we're brother and sister, even though we have different last names," laughed Alejandro.

Javier moved a little closer to Isabela and put his arm around her. "I didn't realize that we were helping you play a practical joke on everyone."

Alejandro and Alicia didn't bother to reply. They just moved forward in line, but Isabela couldn't help but notice that neither teen seemed disturbed that their parents were holding hands.

Chapter 16

For the remainder of the trip, Isabela and Javier talked. He held her hand and gently caressed her arm while they visited about anything and everything. Isabela couldn't remember a time when she had felt so comfortable just talking to someone. The warmth she felt in her chest seemed to spread to her entire body. She wondered if Javier felt it too; if he felt as strongly connected to her as she did to him.

When the bus finally pulled into the parking lot at Richfield High School, it was almost three in the morning. Exhausted teens climbed out of the bus. Many of them had cars parked in the parking lot. Others had called parents to come and pick them up. A few asked Alicia and Alejandro for rides.

A general confusion pervaded the parking lot as teens looked for and located their luggage and instruments and decided how they were going to get home. Isabela was busy getting her van warmed up and the ice scraped off the windshield while various kids loaded their stuff in the back of the vehicle.

Some of the South Sevier kids got out and helped load cars and repack the luggage that needed to remain with the bus. Once the Richfield kids were unloaded, the bus would get back on the freeway and take the South Sevier kids to their high school in Monroe, ten minutes away.

In the confusion of unloading and reloading, Isabela didn't get a chance to say goodbye to Javier. Before she knew it, her van was filled with exhausted teenagers, anxious to get home, and Javier's SUV was no where in sight.

She felt a pang of disappointment that she didn't get to say goodbye, that she didn't at least get to ask him if he would be calling her sometime. Of course, he would call her. He didn't seem like the type to hold hands with a woman and then never contact her again. For a brief moment, Isabela panicked when she realized that he had never asked her for her number, but then she relaxed. He already had her number. They'd exchanged numbers the first day as chaperones.

Once everyone was delivered to their houses, Isabela and Alicia went to their own home. They dragged their suitcases inside the house and abandoned them in the living room next to the front door. Exhausted, they both decided to go to bed and worry about unpacking the following day.

As Isabela drifted off to sleep, she thought about how comfortable she felt with Javier. She couldn't believe there had ever been a time when she disliked him. Now, she wanted to spend all her time with him. She couldn't wait until he called her or texted her. She wondered when that would be. Probably later on in the day she decided.

Except that when she woke up several hours later, she didn't have any texts or missed calls from him. All day, Isabela waited for a call or text, but none came.

Perhaps he was just tired, she reasoned. Or maybe he thought Isabela was too tired, and he was giving her the day to recuperate from the trip. That was it she decided. He was just giving them both time to recover. He would call or text on Monday.

Except he didn't. And he didn't contact her on Tuesday or Wednesday either. Isabela considered asking Alicia if she knew what was going on with Javier, but she didn't want to involve her daughter.

Part of her felt like Alicia had enough worries without worrying about her mother's love life. The other part of her felt embarrassed. What if Javier wasn't interested in her after all? Or what if he'd remembered his vow never to get involved with another woman? Or what if he remembered how rude Isabela had been and decided he didn't want to get involved with someone like that. The what ifs rained all about her, and he still didn't contact her.

By Wednesday evening, Isabela wondered if she should contact Javier. Her mother had raised her to be old fashioned. She felt like it should be the guy doing the chasing. However, they were living in the 21st century. Things were different now than they were when her mother was a kid. Maybe Isabela should take the initiative. She decided to give Javier one more day. If he hadn't contacted her by Thursday night, she would text him.

When Thursday night arrived, she pulled up his number and considered what to text. Maybe he had just been busy getting his book finished by the deadline, she told herself. Maybe if she texted him, it would distract him from his work. She decided to give him another day.

On Friday, she was ready to text him when it occurred to her that since it was the weekend, maybe he already had plans. Maybe she should wait until Sunday night to text. That way if he was busy with friends or relatives, she wouldn't be interrupting anything.

When Sunday rolled around, Isabela told herself that she really would text him, but then she couldn't think what to say. None of the texts she typed out seemed to fit, so she ended up erasing them. *Hi! Remember me? We chaperoned together.* Too Lame. *Hey! How's it going?* Too casual. *Hey Javier, this is Isabela. Why haven't you called me?* Too accusatory. *Hey, is everything all right? I haven't heard from you, so I was worried.* Too familiar. *Hey, I miss you.* Way too forward.

Finally, Isabela gave up. She'd sleep on it and contact him tomorrow.

But when tomorrow arrived, Isabela realized that she wasn't going to get in touch with him, not by phone call and not by text. It was Monday. They'd been home for over a week now. He could have contacted her, but he hadn't. Obviously, he wasn't interested. She'd been nothing more than a fling for him…if you could call holding hands a fling. They hadn't even kissed! But whatever it was, he hadn't cared enough to contact her. And now so much time had passed, if she contacted him, it would make her seem desperate.

Sadly, Isabela replaced her phone on its charger. She had really started to like Javier, but it seemed that maybe her first impression of him was accurate. He really was a jerk. She had trusted him enough to let her heart start to feel something, and he had broken it. Angrily, Isabela brushed away the tears that threatened to fall. She had been happy and contented when it was just her and Alicia, and she would be happy and contented again. She didn't need Javier or any other man for that matter. She steeled her heart and turned her attention to a new book she'd been wanting to read. A book by a different author, not one by him. She didn't want to be reminded of him ever again.

Chapter 17

"Are you and Javier going to start dating?" asked Alicia one day about a week and a half after the trip.

"I don't think so," Isabela replied.

"Why not? You two looked so cute when you were holding hands," said Alicia.

"I don't think he was actually that interested," said Isabela. "I think he just wants us to be friends."

"Friends? Are you kidding me, Mom?" exclaimed Alicia. "He held your hand!"

"Friends hold hands," said Isabela weakly.

"Friends do not hold hands," Alicia stated firmly. "At least, not the way you two were. Trust me. Alejandro and I have been best friends for almost two years now, and we have never held hands."

"What's the deal with you and Alejandro," said Isabela, in an effort to switch the attention to something else. "Why haven't you two dated?"

"Mom, stop trying to change the subject," said Alicia.

"Okay, okay, but I really am curious. Answer that question, and then we can go back to the original topic," said Isabela.

"We're more like brother and sister than boyfriend/girlfriend," explained Alicia. "It's weird. I think Alejandro is handsome, and he thinks I'm cute, but the chemistry just isn't there. We just think of each other as really good friends or misplaced siblings."

"Misplaced siblings," said Isabela. "I like that description."

"So did we," said Alicia. "I think Alejandro is the one who came up with it. We just feel like we should have been brother and sister, twins maybe, but somehow we got misplaced and ended up just friends or something."

"I had a best guy friend in high school also," said Isabela. "The chemistry wasn't there between us to date, but we loved hanging out together."

"Exactly," said Alicia. "And now, tell me what's going on between you and Javier."

"Nothing," Isabela said. "He never texted me or called me, so I'm assuming that means he changed his mind."

"Well, did you text him? Maybe he was waiting for you to make the next move," Alicia challenged.

"I can't do that," said Isabela. "Your grandmother raised me to be old fashioned. She always told me that the guy should do most of the chasing."

"Mom, things are different now. You need to do a little bit of chasing," Alicia pointed out.

"Maybe so," Isabela admitted softly, "but now I feel like it's been too long. I'm not going to text him or call him. If he was really interested, he would have contacted me."

"But what if he was waiting for you?" Alicia protested.

"It doesn't matter," said Isabela. "I don't want to be with a guy that I have to chase. I want someone who is willing to make the effort to chase me. I guess Javier just isn't that guy. Now let's talk about something else."

Alicia started to say something but thought better of it. Instead, she enlisted her mom's help with her math homework, but for the rest of the evening Isabela felt distracted. If she was honest, she missed Javier. She wished she had texted him in the beginning, but now so much time had passed she didn't dare. Her relationship with him was over before it even started.

The next day at work, Isabela received a text from Mr. Jacobs. *Can you chaperone a dance that the music department is sponsoring as a fundraiser Friday night? Please?*

Isabela paused a moment before answering. She didn't have anything going on, but chaperoning a dance sounded kind of overwhelming to her. Much worse than chaperoning a music trip with just a few students. The dances at the high school were usually well attended. She wasn't sure what she would do if she saw two students making out or dancing too closely to each other.

Finally, she replied. *I'm not sure. What would I have to do? I'm a little nervous about what my duties would be.*

A moment later, she received an answering text. *You won't be the only chaperone. I'll have three or four other parents there, plus me and my wife. You just have to circulate. The kids usually behave if we have plenty of adults in the gym.*

Okay, she replied. *What time do I need to be there?*

From 7 to 11 came the reply. *Thanks! You're a life saver!*

Over the next couple of days, Isabela found she wasn't dreading chaperoning the dance after all. Zoe would be chaperoning also. Ever since her niece had disappeared on the music trip, Zoe and Isabela had started to develop a friendship. The dance wouldn't be as bad with Zoe there to talk to.

Miranda was doing much better since the trip to Idaho. She and Zoe were meeting with a counselor and communication between them was improving considerably. Miranda's consequences for disappearing while on the school trip weren't as severe as they could have been. The principal took into account the extenuating circumstances surrounding Miranda. However, she was kicked off the next school trip which was a ski trip to Brianhead Ski Resort in Parowan, Utah. Miranda was understandably disappointed. After spending her entire life in Phoenix, this would have been her first ski trip, but she knew the consequences were fair.

Friday evening, Isabela parked her van in the school parking lot just a few minutes before seven. The dance wasn't scheduled to begin until 7:30, but Mr. Jacobs wanted the chaperones there early.

When Isabela walked into the gym, she was flustered to see Javier already there. He was standing off to the side visiting with another set of parents. He glanced up and saw her and then immediately looked away. Isabela pulled out her phone and pretended to be answering a text. If she had known that Javier would be here, she never would have agreed to chaperone.

A couple of minutes later, Zoe arrived, giving Isabela someone to talk to, but she still felt uncomfortable with Javier in the same room as her. The tension in the air was almost palpable. For a brief moment, Isabela toyed with the idea of pretending she was sick and going back home, but she knew she couldn't do that to Mr. Jacobs.

Fortunately, students began arriving and then Isabela was busy enough circulating around the gym that she didn't have to think about Javier. Every now and then she would see him as he wandered around the gym, but enough students were at the dance that she managed to avoid him.

About an hour into the dance, Alicia sought out Isabela. "Mr. Jacobs is wondering if you would be willing to do an outside sweep of the building with one of the other chaperones," she yelled above the music.

"What's a sweep?" asked Isabela.

"You just go outside and make sure that all the students are inside the building, not hanging around outside smoking or something. It's not that big of a deal. If you see kids out there, you just tell them they need to go inside or go home, but in this cold, no one's ever out there."

"Okay," agreed Isabela. "Do I need to find another chaperone to go with me?"

"No, Mr. Jacobs already found someone. They're out in the entrance where all the trophies are right now," replied Alicia.

Isabela smiled at her daughter and made her way to the entryway. As she stepped out of the dimly lit gym, her mouth dropped open in astonishment. Javier was the other chaperone who had been chosen to help her.

"I'll go see if someone else can join you," she told him coldly.

"Don't bother," he replied. "I'll just do the sweep alone."

At that moment, Alicia and Alejandro came out of the gym. One look at their parents let them know that things were not going well between them.

"You two at least need to discuss things," said Alejandro wisely.

"Yes, you're behaving like a couple of high school kids who got their feelings hurt," said Alicia.

"And we would know because we're in high school," added Alejandro.

"If you two are going to hate each other, fine, go ahead and hate each other," said Alicia, "but at least know why you're mad."

Isabela started to protest, but Alejandro held up a hand to stop her. "Alicia and I are best friends. It's hard on us when our parents don't get along."

"Besides, Mom," spoke up Alicia, "you're always saying that if you do something wrong, you'd like to know what it is so you can fix it. I think most people feel that way. So…we brought you out here to talk things out."

"So, we don't need to sweep the parking lot?" asked Javier stiffly. In spite of the anger she felt towards him, Isabela couldn't help but notice how handsome he looked."

"No, you still need to do that," said Alejandro. "Mr. Jacobs was looking for volunteers, so we volunteered you."

Isabela inhaled sharply. "Why would you volunteer us when you knew we weren't getting along?"

"How would we know you're not getting along? You haven't said three words to each other since you got here. It's obvious you're avoiding each other," Alejandro answered.

"Look," said Alicia gently. "For a long time now, Alejandro and I have talked about getting you two together, but we could never figure out how to do it."

"Until Honor Band came up," said Alejandro. "Mr. Jacobs said he needed a male and a female chaperone, so we volunteered you two. We figured it was a perfect way for you guys to get to know each other."

"And you were getting along so good. You were such a cute couple," put in Alicia. "We don't know what went wrong, but from what you guys have told me and Alejandro, you don't know what went wrong either."

"So, when Mr. Jacobs was looking for more chaperones for the dance, we volunteered you guys, but you kept avoiding each other," said Alejandro.

"And so, you volunteered us again when Mr. Jacobs needed someone to do a sweep outside? Or did you make that part up?" asked Javier. It was difficult for Isabela to determine if he was irritated with the kids or impressed with their ingenuity.

"We volunteered you," said Alejandro.

"But if the sweep hadn't come up, we'd have made something up," added Alicia.

"We're going back into the dance now," said Alejandro. "There's a really cute girl that Alicia is trying to set me up with."

"It's up to you now," said Alicia over her shoulder as they re-entered the gym. "At least try to talk."

Isabela and Javier stood gazing silently at each other, unsure what to say. Finally, Javier broke the silence. "I guess we should start by doing the sweep of the parking lot."

Isabela nodded silently. She slipped on her coat and waited for Javier to do the same. Once they were both bundled up, he opened the door for her, and they stepped out into the cold. About six inches of ice and snow covered the ground. Javier quietly reached down and took Isabela's hand. He tucked it securely in the crook of his arm so that he could help her safely traverse the parking lot. In spite of the ill feelings between them, Isabela felt a surge of warmth. This man was who she wanted to be with, even when she was angry with him.

The pair walked in silence for several minutes until finally Isabela blurted out, "Why didn't you ever call me or text me?"

Javier stopped walking and turned and faced her with a look of pure astonishment. "I did! Several times. You didn't answer any of them, until the very last text I sent. Then you told me to leave you alone and never text you again."

"I never received any texts from you," said Isabela.

"But I texted you!" insisted Javier. "Look! I'll show you."

He pulled out his phone and opened up his texts. Isabela saw that her name had a heart next to it. She did a quick intake of breath. He really did care for her! Javier opened the messages he had sent, each one unanswered until the end when someone had told him to stop texting.

"I never got any of those messages," said Isabela softly. "And I certainly never told you to stop texting me. I don't know how that happened."

Javier took Isabela's hand and they continued walking along the edge of the deserted parking lot. "I think I do," he admitted finally. "The night we got home, I dropped my phone in the parking lot and broke it. I couldn't replace it until Monday, so that's why I didn't contact you the first day."

"And then Monday, you got a new phone?" asked Isabela.

"Yes, but my contacts hadn't been backed up for a while. Since you were a new contact, your info didn't transfer over. I asked Alejandro for your number. I must have put it in wrong," he concluded.

"What number do you have for me?" asked Isabela curiously.

Javier opened up his phone and read the number to her. Isabela smiled slightly. "You have the four and the five reversed. It should be five-four at the end, not four-five."

"So, all this time, I've been texting a total stranger," Javier shook his head in disbelief. "No wonder they told me to leave them alone."

"You know," Isabela giggled, "you have a pretty bad habit of getting yourself into trouble because you have the numbers wrong. First, the hotel and now a random stranger."

Javier joined her laughter. "I need someone to help me keep numbers straight. I'm a writer, not a mathematician."

Isabela shivered. "Let's head back to the gym," she suggested. "I don't see anyone out here."

"Sounds good to me." Javier dropped Isabela's hand and put his arm around her, drawing her in closer so that he could help keep her warm.

Once they were back inside, Javier removed his arm from Isabela's shoulders. She felt a sudden emptiness.

"What now?" she asked.

"Well, first, I'm going to fix your number in my phone," he chuckled.

"I have a better idea. I'll send you a text, then you'll have it." she said.

"Why didn't you contact me before?" asked Javier. He removed his parka and placed it on a table near one of the trophy cases.

"I was afraid," Isabela admitted as she shrugged out of her coat and set it on a nearby chair. "When you didn't text or call, I thought maybe I'd imagined that something was between us. I was afraid if I contacted you, I'd be rejected."

"I could never reject you," said Javier softly.

Inside the gym, a slow song started to play. Javier reached out his hand to her. "May I have this dance?"

Isabela went to him. He wrapped his arms around her, and they swayed slowly to the music. "I didn't realize our kids were such matchmakers," she said softly.

"I'm glad they are," he admitted.

"Me too," she agreed.

She gazed up into his dark eyes. She had never felt so contented, so happy and safe. "What are we going to do with them?" she asked with a smile.

"I think," he said, "that we should give them what they want."

He bent his head towards her and kissed her gently on the lips.

The End